Love Monkeys & Other Stories

Jim Schwartz

DonHanna Press
Los Angeles 2019

Copyright © 2019 Jim Schwartz
All rights reserved

Author photo and book design: Baz Here

Cover art: Baz Here

Other than brief quotations in a review, no part of this book may be reproduced without written permission of the publisher or copyright holder.

ISBN: 9781091285804

DonHanna Press
245 S Serrano Ave
Suite 313
Los Angeles, California 90004 USA

Printed in the United States of America

*To my parents, Doris and Marty,
who I love more with each passing day.*

CONTENTS

SMITTY 9
STUFFED ANIMALS 11
LIVE AND LEARN 13
THE NEED OF WATER 17
THE AMENDS 19
THE PICNIC 22
LOVE MONKEYS 26
BLUEPRINTS 27
THE LONG HAUL 29
A BETTING FOOL 34
THE SQUIRREL 37
THE LOAN 40
THE INTERLOPER 42
RISING FORTUNES 44
GOD'S INSTRUCTIONS TO THE LUSTING MAN 46
DATE NIGHT 48
TWO RABBIS 51
DEATH MASTERS 53
EARL 55
EGGS 60
A NOTE TO ATHEISTS 62
FLEZBAR THE ALIEN 64
BABY 66
LUCKY 70
JUST DESSERT 76
KINDRED SPIRITS 78
ONE LAST REQUEST 80
LOVE BITE 82
HER 87

THE CAT	92
NICORETTE	95
BONDINI'S PLAN	97
HAPPY BIRTHDAY	100
LIMOUSINE EXPERIENCE	101
SEVEN OF EVERYTHING	105
THE HERO	107
WHITE HOUSE	109
A NIGHT ON THE TOWN	112
MY THERAPY	114
VIOLETS	115
THE GOD PLAN	117
ACCEPTANCE	120
THE SISTERS	122
THE DOCTOR'S PROBLEM	126
REVERENCE	131
THE JUMP	135
GOOD AND PROPER	137
PARABLE	139
TREPIDATION	140
THE GREAT TRUTH	142
DISAPPEARANCE	145
ASIAN GRANDMA	147
FIVE SECRETS	149
THE LOSS	150
HORROR	152
PIANO PLAYER	154
THE DRAGON	156
OUR SON	158

SMITTY

There is a windswept beach in October. On it are you me, and your cool dog, Smitty. I toss him a red Frisbee. He makes a fine leaping catch and runs into the ocean. I see his grey terrier body bobbing on the waves, Frisbee dangling from his mouth. Smitty, you yell running to the edge of the water. You clap your hands, panic in the slaps. Smitty, Smitty. I stand frozen watching the drama. For some reason Smitty is swimming away from us. Can that be? He didn't seem suicidal. I mean, he wasn't my dog so I didn't know his quirks, but Smitty seemed like a normal dog, always wagging his tail and playing. In fact, there were many nights I had a better time with Smitty than with you.

Jimmy, you scream. Jim! I snap out of my trance and join you. Smitty is farther out than I thought, his little body propelled by a stiff wind from the southeast. Honey, do something. You grab my arm. I guess I'm supposed to swim after him. There are no lifeguards on duty and I seem to recall you can't swim. I yank off my clothes and clad in underpants wade into the ocean. It's freezing I scream, as if you'll concur that my discomfort is more important than your dog's life. Jimmy, you shriek. Go! Go! Save Smitty! Please.

Although I have a vague desire to be a hero, my love is of the admiration variety and not the all-consuming passion that would make swimming a half-mile to my death a privilege. Nevertheless, I launch myself and initiate a series of smooth strokes, lifting my head every few seconds to breathe and get a bead on the dog. Part of my brain screams fuck you, Smitty, you're too stupid to save. But I persist and gain on him. His little form bobs in a direct line, maybe a hundred yards away. No trace of the Frisbee. I pick up the pace. All those hours humping away on the treadmill at Bally's have given me decent lung power. Forty, thirty, twenty yards. I am a swimming machine, slicing through the brine, focused, closing in. I look up and Smitty is but an arm's length away. His ears are pinned back, eyes fixed on a distant point as he paddles. He is startled when I grab his collar, but when he sees it's me he goes limp. I tuck him under my left arm, turn and power with my right arm back toward land. Smitty licks my ear and shivers.

After what seems like forever I look up. You're but a pinprick on the shore. I redouble my efforts, but when I look up again I can barely see the outline of the beach. The undertow has taken us out too far. I can't do it one-handed. I sigh and look at my little pal. His eyes are unafraid, only beseeching, trying to tell me something. I release him, he licks my face one final time, swivels and resumes his bizarre journey toward his dog destiny.

For a few moments I tread water, watching him and thinking. I glance over my shoulder toward the shore. A low haze has descended, blotting out the mountains framing the beach. I think of you and our time together and all that sadness, the love with no place to go. So many resentments unexpressed, walls erected, as implacable as the blue green water that swirls about me. Overhead a commercial airliner floats into a blue forever, rousing me from my reverie.

Where in God's name is that fool dog swimming to?

I decide to find out.

STUFFED ANIMALS

A couple of Sundays ago I woke up broke. Since the BK I don't have credit cards. I couldn't get money from my paltry checking account for another ten hours since the previous afternoon I had withdrawn my $300 limit at Hollywood Park and bet it on a toad masquerading as a horse.

I was starving. The only thing in the refrigerator was the bottle of soy sauce that had been there for five years. As I was lifting it to my lips, you called.

We hadn't spoken for a while. I figured you had sex on your mind. After all, that's what we did when we got together every few months or so. I didn't have the energy but a blowjob had a certain allure. That wasn't your style, though. I once fell asleep after you did me first and was awakened by a beer bottle exploding against the wall.

You say why don't we have breakfast and spend the day together. I'm a little short, I say. Oh, Jim, it's the horses again, you poor man. I say something profound like it is what it is. You say you'll pick me up in an hour and we'll go to Norm's.

An hour's a long time when you're out of your mind with hunger. I try to watch TV but after a Doritos, Captain Crunch, and Duncan Hines commercial I turn it off. I shower, shave, and spray Versace perfume onto my privates. Sweet God that burns, it feels like my nuts are in an anthill.

The longest hour ends and you pick me up. You've gained some weight but look cute in your torn jeans and baggy sweatshirt. When we kiss, your lips remind me of someone I once knew.

We get to Norm's and the wait is twenty minutes. Twenty minutes! I could swear most of the folks in Norm's lobby have just eaten. You hand me a bunch of quarters and I play the game with the metal pincers and stuffed animals. I have an insane need to win a stuffed animal for you but the little creatures fall off the hooks as I am about to drop them in the slot.

We get a table, place our order and catch up. The law firm is still killing you. I'm playing the horses. Your mom has been declared dead four times. My mom spends most of her waking moments in Costco, except for the hour she spends in religious communion with *The View*.

When the food arrives, I try to be human, but I'm too hungry. I blaze a burning path through eggs, buttered toast, potatoes, pancakes, all sorts of cooked meats, and the remaining two thirds of your waffle. When I come up for air you're paying the tab.

I pray that you'll drop me off at home so I can watch the Jet game and sleep. Once in the car, however, you rest your hand on my thigh and stroke it. I do deep breathing exercises trying to force air and feeling into my penis but the left side of Norm's menu is blocking it. In the elevator up to your apartment, you put your tongue in my ear and play with my nipples. I'm thinking three Alka Seltzers will do the trick. Once upstairs you go to the bathroom. I head into your bedroom and knock about fourteen stuffed animals off the bed so I can lie down. What an idiot I was, playing that stupid game at Norm's.

The last thing you need is another stuffed animal.

LIVE AND LEARN

When I was twenty-three years old, my quest for fame and fortune brought me to New York City and a job with *Encyclopedia Britannica*. I was a rising star and it wasn't uncommon for me to sell two sets of books a day. I was sharp and knew it.

The way we got leads was by purchasing them from the company. *Britannica* would run ads in magazines, things with clip out coupons. Potential clients would return the coupons and we'd buy them for different amounts, depending on the magazine. For instance, coupons from *Time* or *Life* went for ten bucks because they were mint. I proudly boasted that I never spent more than a buck on a lead, getting mine from such rags as *Throwing Knife News* or *Swat Team Digest*.

I followed one of my cheap leads to the slums of the East Village one sunny fall afternoon. As I walked along Fifth Street most of the buildings were demolished or burned out. But I forged ahead, feeling that I had the power of the ages in the little presentation case that swung at my side.

For you see, and I'm a little embarrassed to admit this, I believed that *Encyclopedia Britannica* was a remarkable educational tool. In my mind, I saw a family of four sprawled before a crackling fire, smiling, and pointing to pictures of vintage cars, American Presidents, or dinosaurs, and being drawn together by all that knowledge. I imagined that when the family started to argue the mother or father would say, "Hold on now, let's take a look at our encyclopedia," and they would, and then everything would be just fine.

I finally reached my appointment's ramshackle building, ascended a series of reeking stairways to the fourth floor, and knocked on a thin door. After about twenty seconds the door opened to reveal a bleary-eyed, balding old guy dressed in nothing but a pair of filthy boxer shorts. I apologized for waking him, told him who I was, and reminded him he had made a presentation appointment. After a few moments, he nodded and motioned me into the apartment. As I walked by, I noticed his chest hair was matted with what appeared to be strawberry jam. Behind me the door slammed shut and several locks clicked into place.

The room looked more like a landfill than an apartment. Piles of newspaper, cartons, clothing, food containers, and unidentifiable bric-a-brac were lined floor to ceiling. A sweet smell hung in the air. He reached behind the pile, withdrew two Samsonite chairs and opened them. I sat down without looking and heard something squish and splatter beneath my butt. With the greatest effort, I kept a smile plastered on my face and vowed that the old man was going to pay for my dry cleaning bill, and more, with his purchase of the leather-bound Italian edition of *Encyclopedia Britannica*.

I opened my case and spread out my presentation. He sat down in the other chair about four feet from me and folded his hairy legs. I glanced at the lead coupon in my hand and got started.

"Mr. Joyner, what can I say, that you'll be happy if you buy a set of *Britannica*? I can't do that, I can't promise happiness. What I can promise is that having a set of *Encyclopedia Britannica* is going to open up your heart and your mind and help you to enjoy life like you never have before." As I spoke he picked his nose with great gusto. I paid him no heed.

"Information is priceless, Bill," I continued, "and we get our information from books. And the best books in the whole universe are *Encyclopedia Britannica*." He leaned back in his chair and I noticed for the first time that for an old guy he was powerfully built. With all that hair, he looked like an ape. He asked if the books could help him win at the racetrack.

"As a matter of fact, we have an instant information program just for questions like that," I replied. "You call a twenty-four-hour hotline and tell 'em what you need. They'll have a full report in your hands the very next day."

He asked if I was bullshitting him. I pointed to one of the colorful posters on the floor. "It's all there," I said. "You can see for yourself. Call our report line and I'll bet—excuse the pun—they can tell you all you need to know about the racetrack. And put down a daily double for me, okay?" He leaned forward.

"Do you believe in the devil?" he asked.

"Gosh," I said. "I don't know. What do you think?" He said he was the devil himself and that young boys like me got his pecker as hard as an old pepperoni.

My stomach did a little somersault. The graphs on the floor looked pretty stupid. I watched in amazement as he pulled his erect penis out of his underpants and shook it at me.

"This," he said, "is all the information you'll ever need, sonny."

"I'm sorry, sir, I think we have a misunderstanding."

"Oh no," he said. "I think a fag boy like you understands just fine."

I leaned forward and began putting the materials back into my case. "Well, thanks for the thought, Mr. Joyner, but I have to be going." I had almost gotten everything loaded when he called, "Ziggy! Verschmacta! Commen ze Ziggy!"

I heard a rustling sound and glanced at the doorway that apparently led to a second room. A huge German Shepherd sat there, teeth bared, eyes glistening with hate. A low growl emanated from deep in its throat.

"You see," said Mr. Joyner, "I'm going to fuck your fat ass and shoot a jizzball into your heart. If you give me any shit the dog'll rip you up."

Never, I thought, would I buy a dollar lead again. Just Park Avenue and Fifth Avenue addresses from here on out.

"I wouldn't enjoy that, Bill," I said. "And don't you think it'd feel better if your partner was into it?"

He blinked. Like there was something in what I said that got through to him. Then he said the weirdest thing, he said, "I was a teacher. I know about books, the classics, Shakespeare. My students enjoyed me … before the voices, that is. But after I got out of the hospital, nobody gave a rat's ass. They fired me and I moved to this shit-hole. You think I enjoy living like this? You think I'm nuts, is that it?"

"No sir. You seem like an okay guy. It's just that I have appointments and I must be going."

I tried to get up and found I was stuck fast to the chair.

"Crazy glue," he said. "Sometimes I use it instead of the handcuffs."

I casually began undoing my belt and unbuttoning my pants. "This is bullshit, Mr. Joyner. I came here with good intentions, to share with you the joys of great books and wisdom and knowledge. And you have the nerve to ruin a good suit because you can't be a gracious host. A former teacher, no less. If anyone should know the value of *Britannica* it's you!"

When I was down to my shorts I eased myself off the chair. I stood up in my suit jacket, shirt, tie, underpants and grabbed my case.

"Have a good day, Mr. Joyner, and thanks for your time."

I never could have guessed what happened next. Because he started laughing. A deep, rich hearty laugh. A belly laugh. The kind you want to join in on. The dog padded over and looked at him with crazy eyes wondering what the hell was happening. But the guy kept on laughing. Tears were coming out of his eyes. He was leaning forward, one arm wrapped around his waist, the other pointing at me, laughing, laughing.

With about as much dignity as a guy in my position could muster, I walked to the door and opened the locks. Suddenly the room was silent. For some reason, I turned around.

He was sitting in the chair staring into space, petting the dog's huge head. The dog's tail was going a mile a minute and the scene looked so normal I had the urge to go in and resume the presentation. Then I glanced at my ruined pants stuck to the chair and ran out.

Outside, I strode down Avenue C in my underpants while guys on stoops whistled and called to me. A merciful cabdriver picked me up.

On the ride uptown, I thought about the experience. At first I was thrilled to be alive. But by the time I got to my apartment I was thinking about what had cost me the sale. It dawned on me that I should have taken more time before going into the pitch. By opening the presentation charts too fast I had rushed the old guy and made him defensive. A little more time with the chit-chat, getting to know his interests and so forth, and I could have had him.

Live and learn, I thought. Live and learn.

THE NEED OF WATER

It was Kentucky Derby day. The inside of his apartment was a mess: used tissues, unread copies of *the New Yorker*, racing papers, underwear, dirty paper plates. He was on his back, on the bed. He needed a new mattress; the thing had become a hammock. An early May sun was a weapon blasting holes through his windows. His cell phone rang. Damn telemarketers.

"Como estas," he said. "No tengo dinero." This usually got rid of them.

"Hello, Robert?" It was the voice of a young woman. Expectation rose in him like a sigh.

"This is Robert."

"It's Rebecca." For a moment, a lack of recognition. Then a flickering of hope.

"Rebecca. Ohmygod, Rebecca, sweetheart, how are you?"

Rebecca was the daughter of the last woman he cared about. Rebecca was six when he met them. That day, he was in his car, they were walking up the street hand in hand, he saw them in the rearview and almost drove off. He stayed for twelve years. He could have been a father but he didn't have it in him, he was too distracted. He wasn't a bad man, just broken.

"I'm fine," Rebecca said. "It's been a while since I've seen you." It had been over a decade. She must be twenty-eight by now. "I was in Europe but now I'm back in the States."

After he and Rebecca's mother parted—it wasn't a breakup so much as a wearing away, an erosion of a fragile substance—he became consumed with his own needs. He was supported by the government. When the checks came, he tore open the envelopes like a small boy the wrappings on Christmas gifts.

"I'd love to see you, Rebecca. Can you meet for coffee? There's a Starbucks on Pico near Robertson."

She agreed and he was given new life. He shaved, showered, tweezed and went through his closet trying to find something that would fit on a body thickened with flab. He sniffed his one pair of sneakers and sprayed them with Right Guard. He posed in front of the mirror. The colors weren't right. He drove too fast, afraid the engine on his old Corolla would overheat. On Pico, old men in loose, button down short-sleeve shirts walked with hands clasped behind their backs. Wide-hipped women in long black skirts pushed babies in strollers staring straight ahead. There was moisture on his palms as he gripped the steering wheel.

She was sitting at the first table. When she stood up, breath whooshed out of him. Her beauty was a magic trick. She had become a woman. He could discern no imperfection, though he tried, it was his way. The hug was brief but promising. She was slim and strong.

Over coffee, they reminisced and smiled. She told him she had no significant other. To desire her wasn't wrong. The relationship with her mother was in the past. He was thinking about asking her to a movie or maybe the horse races.

"One thing I've always wondered," she said.

He was staring at the coffee. He had forgotten the cream. The three of them had a dog for a long time. The dog loved him the most. He was the only one who played with it. Rebecca and her mother babied it, dressed it in silly outfits. He fed it lots of scraps. When it died, they blamed him.

"What's that?" he asked. He looked up. Her eyes spoke of nothing, there was an emptiness. People in LA thought they needed water. That wasn't it.

Rebecca said, "Why didn't you ever love us?"

THE AMENDS

The banker had much to be thankful for. He had money, an attentive, kind wife, and his health was good for a man in his 60's. Yet there burned within him a need to make amends for a misdeed he had committed as a youth.

He had stolen from his first wife. They met in college. She worked part-time in a massage parlor and ensnared him with her sexual prowess and money. She gave him the money she earned for their future. Even then he craved money as a sane man does love. He offered her the promise of legitimacy and was on course to have a brilliant career in his father's bank. He promised that if they were still together in three years he would marry her. It seemed inconceivable but time has a way of baffling those who cling to material things. Just after the three years were up, he kept his promise and married her. Word of her sex work reached his family and they boycotted the wedding. Several months later, shunned by his father and in abject misery, he convinced her that their only chance for happiness was to annul the marriage and begin anew. She agreed as she still trusted him.

Unbeknownst to her, he had succumbed to the gaming tables in Atlantic City. He gambled away the $30,000 she planned for their future. After he lost he made a feeble attempt at suicide by slashing the tops of his wrists with a razor blade. Though bleeding profusely, he was in no mortal danger. His father came to the hospital, talked with his son, and set out a plan for renewal. He sent him to a city in the Midwest where he got counseling, resurrected himself, and went to business school. His father rebuffed the former wife and her attorney until they melted away.

Now, forty years later, the need to make amends had interrupted the peaceful voyage. He discussed his intention with his current wife. She was deferential and trusting. He was hoping she would talk him out of it. That night, in bed, he stroked her hair. It was unusual for him to touch her in bed. They had not had sexual relations in years. Passion had left their relationship. Yet he needed something, a connection he felt sex might provide. He nuzzled against her, kissed her cheek, nibbled her ear. Her flatulent snoring continued unabated. He retreated to his side of the bed and was punished by thoughts of the wet and delicious sex he and his first wife had shared.

He could not find a trace of her. A colleague recommended a private detective. Within a week, the gumshoe had acquired the information. It was worth the large fee.

His former wife was living in New York City. She had never remarried. Her name was legally changed. There were several bankruptcies on her record. She was a nurse at a hospital on Manhattan's Upper West Side and lived in a rundown studio close by.

He withdrew $95,000 from one of his accounts. He placed it in a briefcase. He wanted to be generous in his restitution and include interest on the principal. The night before he flew to New York, he enjoyed a simple meal with his wife. Afterwards, they sat on opposite ends of the couch and watched an old movie.

While on the plane, he pulled up the window guard and was shocked to see ghouls in the innocent clouds, swirling faces of loathing and disgust. He wished he had a faith, a God to whom he could turn. As a child, he had been disgusted by what he perceived as his parents' hypocritical relationship to God. After his confirmation at age sixteen he never again set foot in a house of worship.

When the plane landed at JFK, he felt as if he had run a marathon. He had two quick beers at the first bar he could find. On the ride in from the airport he looked out the window at the small, nondescript homes jammed one against the other. He wondered how anybody could be happy in such circumstances. His former wife could not be happy. Her life was a history of defeat. He glanced at the briefcase and felt a surge of righteousness. This money would clear the slate and help her start a new life and obtain fine things.

The hotel room was palatial, a suite with a piano in an anteroom. It was his plan to go to the hospital first thing in the morning. According to the detective, she worked the day shift. He wanted to meet her in a public place. If there was a scene, he wanted his participation to be above reproach.

He slept not at all. As he walked to the hospital he had the sense of losing his moorings.

Passersby sneered at him. A taxicab barely missed him as he meandered across an intersection. He clutched the briefcase containing the amends money as if it was a lover's hand. When he spied the canopy of the hospital, tightness crept up his spine. It moved to his throat and constricted it. He grabbed at his tie, yanked it, and tore at the buttons on his shirt. He sank to his knees, breath rasping, throat swelling, and toppled over, head slamming onto the pavement.

He awoke in the ICU. As his eyes swam into focus he saw a familiar face inches from his own. He knew at once it was his former wife. He tried to speak but could only whisper as he had a thick tube running out of his throat.

"Relax, darling," she said.

"I have money for you, that is why I have come. Did they give you the briefcase?"

"Yes, I have the briefcase," she said.

"Good," he said. "Good."

"It was very thoughtful of you," she said. "But what of my innocence? What of my faith, my dreams? The hate that has consumed me? What of my life?"

She filled a syringe with an amber fluid he knew was poison. She held it close to his arm. For a moment horror engulfed him. Then, as we all must, he acceded to the final moment as she injected him with the lethal dose.

At almost the same moment the banker's wife was roused from her yoga workout. At the door were two local detectives. They informed her that her husband had died the previous night at a hotel in New York City. It was a massive heart attack. There was no evidence of foul play. They wondered what he was doing with a briefcase filled with so much money.

THE PICNIC

Somehow, I'd gotten into the corporate picnic business. That meant that every Saturday and Sunday during the summer I did the catering and ran the games for hundreds of employees of the largest corporations in Southern California. Most of the time the events went well. Oh, every once in a while, there'd be a problem. Once a clown I hired had a nervous breakdown and ran through the crowd yelling "you suck" and throwing water balloons at the guests. And another time a propane tank exploded, sending about a thousand hot dogs whizzing through the air like tracer bullets. But by and large the events were sedate affairs, characterized by plenty of good food, games, and a nice day in a California park.

One day I was doing such an event at a park in Chino, in the heart of dairy country. The air was redolent with the smell of fresh cow shit but that wasn't the major problem. The problem was the flies, big hairy bastards the size of sparrows, that flew around landing on everybody and crawling all over the food. I had my employees fanning towels at the food stations in a vain attempt to keep the flies away. But they kept coming, like demented soldiers on a fool's mission.

It being a picnic, most of the picnic-goers had a high tolerance for things like flies, having the attitude that, like ants, flies came with the territory. For those few who were faint of heart I kept a calm veneer and assured them that everything was fine and the flies were harmless, all the while bobbing and weaving and smacking the flies off my face with the flat of my hand.

Heading into the critical part of the afternoon, everything was going well. The crowd was chowing down on chili-dogs, chicken, potato salad, ice cream, and having a good old time. I was just about to set up the table for Bingo when an ashen faced employee named Teresa staggered up to me.

"Th-th-th-th ..." she stammered.

"What, Teresa, spit it out," I said. "What's the problem?"

"Th-th-th-there's a ... lady in the bathroom and .... Y-y-you have to come quick."

I tensed but made certain I kept a broad smile on my face, for the first rule of catering is never let the client see that anything is wrong.

Ever. The cooks didn't show up? Keep smiling. The meat is rancid, the ice cream has melted? Ha ha ha. A large rat just jumped off the truck and the beer permits are invalid? No problem, just keep on smiling, no matter what.

Once I'd gotten Teresa out of sight, I asked what was wrong. Her face was as white as my BVD's and she was having trouble working her lips. She grabbed my hand and led me to the women's restroom, which was, thankfully, far from the dining area. When we reached the entrance, she kept pulling me, as if she intended to lead me inside. What could have happened inside the woman's restroom that required my attention? I was filled with dread and curiosity.

The restroom seemed to be empty. Once inside, Teresa moved by herself to the far stall and stood before it, hand clasped to her mouth. I edged behind her and saw the object of her terror. It was the most remarkable thing I'd ever seen in my life. For there, sitting on the pot, was a creature with the body of a woman and the head of a fly. The head was huge, larger than a human's, with antennae waving around. And words were coming out of the fly-mouth.

"I just came in to move my bowels," it said in a voice that was half buzz and half that of a mature woman, "and then I got this horrible headache. I don't know how long I was here. But when I was finished I went out to put on lipstick and saw … that … and saw … my God! I've turned into a damn fly, haven't I?"

She was remarkably calm for someone who had just transformed into an insect the size of a condor.

"Yes," I said, "it seems as if you have." I touched her head to see if some practical joke was being played. The skin was warm and viscous and protoplasmic, and it wasn't a mask.

"We've got to get her out here," Teresa shrilled. "We've got to get her to a hospital."

What's a hospital going to do for her, I thought? And anyway, who has insurance to cover being turned into a fly? No, I could see taking her to a large pile of fresh dung and letting her forage for corn kernels, but not to a hospital.

My main concern was to keep the discovery from the picnic-goers, for it would frighten them and disrupt the picnic. The key was to get through Bingo, the water balloon toss, and the egg toss and have the afternoon be declared a success. You see, I was terrified of not getting paid.

"I'm sorry," I could see the client saying, "but nowhere in our contract was it specified that a disgusting, large fly would appear and frighten my employees. I don't feel our company has to pay for such treatment." I had to keep a lid on this in order to get through the day.

"Look," I said to the fly-lady, "I've seen this kind of thing before. It happened at a picnic in Irwindale. A little boy turned into a hornet for about an hour. He stung a park ranger, but it wasn't a big deal. He changed back during the park clean up. I think the same thing's happening to you. Just stay cool and everything will work out."

"Maybe," said the fly-lady, "I should go and tell my husband and children, just so they know where I am."

"I wouldn't want him to see me like that if I were you," I said. "It might change ... the way he *feels*." Her shrieks and buzzes of grief were heart-rending but I had a picnic to get through.

"Maybe you're right," she nodded.

"Of course, I am," I replied. "Now, Theresa, you stay with ..."

"Mrs. Boyer," the fly-lady said.

"Mrs. Boyer. Get her anything she needs. A piece of garbage, a piece of raw chicken, anything. I'll come back later and I'm sure everything will be okay."

They both nodded. I pushed a resisting Theresa into the stall and shut the door behind her. I glanced at my watch. Three o'clock. Two more hours and I'd be fine.

I found Mr. Boyer and told him his wife was ill and had gone for a stroll. He looked perplexed as I smiled and went to the Bingo table. Within minutes everybody had a Bingo card and was ready to play the first game for a lovely cutlery set.

The games went smoothly for I was a wonderful Bingo caller. Being a wild gambler, I could feel the demon need in the people and played it like an instrument. By the time we were in our sixth game and playing for an Electric Lint Brush, the crowd was whipped into a fever pitch.

I had just called "B-9" when I heard a shrill scream coming from the direction of the woman's bathroom. I fiddled with the Bingo balls, withdrew one, and called "N-37" when a louder, closer scream raked the air. I looked up to see Teresa running towards us, blouse ripped to shreds and hair a mess.

Lumbering behind her, with antennae waving and on legs that were half-human and half those of a hairy fly, came Mrs. Boyer. In slow motion, I saw the group rise as one.

"Please," I yelled through a big smile, "the next number is 0-72 and don't forget we're playing for a lovely and valuable electric utensil!"

It wouldn't have mattered if we were playing for the Hope Diamond. The damage had been done and the crowd was on their feet and running in all directions. Mrs. Boyer made a beeline—excuse the expression—for Mr. Boyer and pinned him up against the side of a cabana with her proboscis.

"It's me, honey," she buzzed. "It's me, Lois." Mr. Boyer's tongue lolled to the side of his mouth and his eyes fluttered. "Please," she continued, "you must help me."

He managed to duck out of her grasp and sprint with the rest of the picnickers toward the parking lot. Mrs. Boyer hadn't mastered flying yet and wriggled along in a vain attempt to catch him. I watched the parking lot as cars banged into one another as people tried to get away.

I slumped to a bench with a sigh. Well, I'd done everything I could to make the picnic a success. Just another lesson in humility, another taste of my infinite powerlessness.

"Hey mister," I heard a young voice call, "what's the next number? I'm still playing." I looked up to see a young boy, maybe twelve, sitting at a table with three or four Bingo cards spread in front of him.

"What are you doing here, son? Aren't you afraid?"

"Nah," he shrugged. "I've seen *The Fly* maybe a hundred times. It's no big deal."

I had to smile. What a trooper, what a kid. Too bad he wasn't the client.

"Well, of course we can still play Bingo," I said. "And son, I have a feeling you're going to win some mighty fine prizes."

"Great," he said. "I'll give some to my mom. Then maybe she won't feel so bad about turning into a fly."

LOVE MONKEYS

I wasn't supposed to be playing around with the animals. I was hired to feed and water them. But late at night when I was all alone and the only sounds were those of the refrigeration units and the fluorescent lights, it was hard not to want to play with the monkeys. So I did.

I took them out of their cages, careful that the wires leading from outlets in their heads and necks didn't strangle them. I gave them bananas and candy bars and let them stroll around the laboratory. One night I brought in my CD player and a large orange monkey and I danced to the beat of a Madonna song. I led.

I don't know if you'd call it love at first sight, but the orange monkey and I began to have a thing for one another. She'd see me coming and set up a terrific chatter until I let her out of the cage. Each night as we danced, she'd press her warm, furry body closer to me. When she first stuck her tongue in my ear I was horrified. But I got to like it.

Before long we were exploring each other's bodies with our hands and mouths. We finally had intercourse on a Wednesday night. I remember it was a Wednesday because I went to my regular Codependents Anonymous meeting before coming into work. It was on top of the long autopsy table. As I plunged my cock into the little beast her shrieks filled the air, making me wonder if I wasn't too large for her. But she wouldn't let me go, so I assumed it was OK. Of course, I wore a condom.

One night when I came into work her cage was empty. I figured they had moved her to a different laboratory until I saw her head floating in a big jar of preservative. I repressed the urge to cry and was glad that at no time in the relationship had we made a commitment. Then the pain would have been unbearable.

For several nights I went through the motions of my job. To tell you the truth, I was devastated. But after a proper period of mourning, perhaps a week, an albino rhesus monkey caught my eye as I was emptying the wastepaper baskets.

She was smaller than the orange monkey but very firm.

BLUEPRINTS

You get to a point in your life. It's all new or it better be. Things get colorless, they become interesting. Love has something to do with it. Or not. It might be a dream fueled adventure involving immortality. Or so it seems. Maybe they badgered you about your blueprints. Something was amiss. Maybe you were too smart or there was an element of cad about you. Not that you were trying to stack the deck, magnetize the dice, arrange the planets to increase fortune on your venture, your mad mind meld, your stupid little grinning private joke, do you know what I mean? Are you getting my drift, Seymour, God of light and substance? So, you check into your hotel room, shower, open the money bar, and call a girl up to the room. Like everything else it seems like the real deal, the Squantum love nest, folding phallus into dove swallows, mirrored images of flagellated love songs flying east to a lonely horizon and you go along. After all, you can give up dreams as easily as anybody. It's about letting go. Or having whatever holds you let go and maybe a bit of adversity, a Skin Bracer slap upside the head, a boulder in a river creating a miraculous tributary and a new civilization. Small solace that the quick and tricky slick chick that knocked thrice on your hotel wood is herself a seeker of squalor masquerading as time or the most real of real. And when your lips meet and she lets you feel her, feel her, you're prepared to play God and I know this because I have felt the innocence of no trying, the act of submission before caring most pure, when all is intelligence before wisdom. She unzips your fly as planes float in the blue outside your Marriott window and it's too bright, too bright. Although her manicured nails are long and pointy it doesn't hurt when she touches. It fact, it's as soft as the sheets on the bed and her perfume enfolds you in the no-care zone, a dangerous place where even immortals fear to tread. And you lie back, you tumble into the softness of your resignation and it is a time unexplored but evident in your blueprints. Do you like to travel, she asks? Travel? Exploration is all, it is the beginning and end of humanity, it is creationary. And hey, it musta been a helluva night, you know what I mean, cause when you wake up and you've missed your flight, whoa, you kinda don't care, she was sumpin' wasn't she? With no wallet, you wander the airport checking newspapers for the date. You expect to kick past this rocky time, stone ramped steep down cascading rapids, cartwheeling, careening, split from want and data like your edgy friend who exists as hope and memory indistinguishable and glowing. And where are your corporate fellows come to collect you? Come to examine your clothes, your ideas, your fabrications? At least you've got your hat. And it's outside the store with the little alligators on pastel shirts and where people are consuming huge mounds of breakfast foods at tables so white they appear surgical that they ask for your identification. Love is immutable you tell the steely eyed representative of Homeland Security. If I had my blueprints you'd understand, you say. The evidence. The truth. The things that will set us free! Let us embrace this nascent moment of undoing, Mr. Blue Suited Agent, and as they lead you away you see the Marriott girl running down the corridor toward you, and in her hands is the answer, the calling of humans: a God of faith of reason, of things unspoken and profound.

THE LONG HAUL

After being in the mental institution for the better part of six months, Jack Lewis was losing hope of ever getting out. He was having trouble pretending he was well, and the doctors knew he was having trouble pretending, which was too bad, because he actually *was* well.

Except for the 400 milligrams of Thorazine four times a day, which turned him into a slab of quartz, Lewis felt good. He had hope for the future. He couldn't wait to move back into his dumpster and win at the horse races.

Lewis had gained quite a bit of weight, almost ninety pounds, due to a steady diet of stewed peaches, pudding, bread, butter, pizza, and ice cream. His reflexes were a little slow. For instance, it was hard to get toothpaste to land on the brush in the mornings. He missed several times before it squiggled onto the bristles. If he dropped soap in the shower, it took a while to pick it up. Later he would find out he was losing his sense of touch because of the medication. Thorazine was developed by Sandoz in the late 1950's. They were looking for a medication that would pacify the inmates at Alcatraz. When they gave Thorazine to lab monkeys and saw the creatures peel bananas, stick them in their ears, and start chewing, they knew they hit pay dirt.

It was on the day that Lewis finally gave up hope of getting out that he decided to kill his shrink, Dr. Miles Yudim. He wasn't a shrink so much as a pipe smoking, suit-wearing pile of shit. He had about as much charisma as a couch, and that's doing a couch a disservice. For months, patient Lewis thought the little smile Yudim wore meant he was appreciating his grand tales of progress. He finally realized it was a grimace produced by the Dr. holding his pipe in a steady position.

The only word Dr. Yudim uttered in his 150 sessions was "So?" and he let that fly about twelve times a session. Lewis felt anyone would be maddened by a shrink who muttered "So" instead of actually conversing. It was unfortunate that it was around that time that Lewis made the decision to kill Dr. Yudim, because they were close to sending him home.

There was some question as to where home was. Lewis's previous address was a dumpster on the corner of Alameda and 14th Street. It was outside of a leather goods manufacturer. The employees weren't permitted to dump food products in the dumpster, just remnants from the shoes and belts they produced. The dumpster was lined with layers of the softest leather and smelled like a new car. Quiet, safe, and cost efficient.

Lewis enjoyed that unique lifestyle. In any event, he had no income or friends, and his parents had sought restraining orders against him for years. At first, he had to keep fifty yards away. Now it was three miles. Lewis tried to respect his parents' wishes but broke down every Thanksgiving and showed up with a pumpkin pie. It was the last visit that landed him in this hellhole. He insisted his father was trying to punch him, and he had nothing to do with the fall, and his father's subsequent paralysis.

As the idea to kill the shrink became palpable, Lewis toyed with the idea of sharing his plan with Nurse Frankel. She was the most beautiful woman he had ever met. He liked women in uniforms. He and Nurse Frankel would go on for hours about how phony everything was at the hospital. She would hold his hand and tell him about her rescue dogs. One day Lewis told her about a lanyard he was making in arts and crafts. A special, extra-large lanyard. She complimented him on his newfound interest in hospital activities. He didn't pursue his plan.

When Lewis was escorted in for his next session, he decided to stop pretending all was well. He mentioned his discontent.

Dr. Yudim said: "So?"

"So," Lewis said, "you're an Israeli turd and I'd love to yank your eyes out. I'm tired of you and this shithole and I want to go back to my dumpster."

Lewis thought he saw something flicker in Dr. Yudim's eyes. Maybe just a tendril of smoke proving a momentary annoyance. For the first time Yudim sat forward.

"So?"

"So," he said, "if you say "so" one more time I won't be responsible for my actions. I know you were in the Israeli army, Pancho. But I'm not some eight-year-old Palestinian kid with a rock."

Lewis knew his speech was like a prisoner telling a parole board that he was ready to resume killing. Fuck it. He had to take a stand.

Dr. Yudim leaned forward, tapped his pipe in the ashtray. "So?"

Lewis took the lanyard out of his pocket and flexed it. "I made this for you," he said. "What do you think? Should I have used more teal?" He snapped the cord a couple of times.

"So?" said Dr. Yudim.

"Leave the gun, take the canoli," Lewis snarled and leaped over the desk. Because of the Thorazine, the leap took the better part of a minute. Lewis saw Dr. Yudim's hand whip out of his pocket, a stun gun held in it. In the next moment, Lewis felt as if he had stuck his cock into an electrical wall outlet. His eyeballs became jumbo eggs, fried over easy. His last thought before losing consciousness: Thorazine does not facilitate physical dexterity.

When Lewis came to, he was in his room in a straightjacket. Nurse Frankel was by his side, a small cup of drug-laced pineapple juice in her hand. She dabbed his head with a wet towel.

"Don't try to move," she said. "They have you trussed up pretty good." She proffered the medication. Lewis was so thirsty he didn't mind the incipient Thorazine-induced numbness.

"I did it," he said.

"Did what?"

"It doesn't matter," he said. "I'll be here forever. Maybe we can get married."

"Hello?"

"It's not a bad idea. We can be happy here."

"It's the drugs talking."

"Whatever. You're the woman for me."

"That's because I'm the only woman under sixty years old in this place."

"Whatever. We'll have a wedding feast in the cafeteria. All the stewed peaches you can eat."

"How romantic."

"Help me out of this straitjacket. It'll be your initial commitment."

"That's not a great word under the circumstances. What happened in Dr. Yudim's office?"

"I can't explain it," I said. "I think I tried to strangle him."

"No!"

"With a lanyard. Until he tased me."

"You tried to *kill* Dr. Yudim?"

"Maybe. Who knows. Once we're married it'll make more sense."

"You poor baby," she murmured. Lewis thought she kissed him. A deep, rich kiss. But he might have been dreaming.

Dr. Yudim and Nurse Frankel met in his office later that night.

"He asked you to marry him?"

"Yes."

"He's an interesting case. I never would have guessed him to be so decisive."

"What do you plan to do with him?"

Dr. Yudim struck a match and held it against the bowl of cherry pipe tobacco. He leaned back in his chair and regarded the twisted, snow-covered branches quivering outside his office window.

"I don't know," he said. "The lad has emotional problems. After all, his only goals seem to be moving back into a dumpster and winning at the horse races. I don't know if I'll ever be able to help him. After all, I have reached just one patient in twelve years of practice."

"Paul Morse?"

"Yes "

"But Morse killed himself on the day he was to be released."

"Morse was cured. The suicide was a technicality."

Dr. Yudim sucked the pipe and closed his eyes.

"I'm thinking of marrying him," said Nurse Frankel. Dr. Yudim opened his eyes.

"Sometimes," he said, "when the snow falls I feel the daffodils trying to push their way to the surface. And when snow swirls and banks and turns everything white and icy, I imagine the songbirds drifting into formations in the deep south, setting their internal compasses for points north. This is how I know that disparate events presage grand, unpredictable occurrences." Nurse Frankel had never heard such a poetic outburst from Dr. Yudim.

"I would counsel against marriage," continued Dr. Yudim. "After all, you are pregnant with our child."

"Lewis and I can raise him."

"In a dumpster?"

"Patient Lewis and the child can live with me."

"I'm not sure how to respond," said Dr. Yudim. "It's rather bizarre from a therapeutic point of view. The lad's a compulsive gambler."

"He's quite good," said Nurse Frankel. "Using the horse entries in the *New York Times* over the past few months, I've watched him turn a paper profit of almost $900."

"Hardly enough to support a family."

"I believe one can live on dreams."

"It's those words that made me fall in love with you, Edith. However, I will not release Lewis. I'm going to wean him off all medication. He's been whining about the Thorazine for months. Then I will teach him the horrors of lost freedom and impossibility of redemption. When I have crippled him, I will give him to you as a gift."

"You're sick in a wise way, Doctor," said Nurse Frankel. She leaned across the desk and kissed his cheek. She ran her fingers through his few strands of hair.

She liked Dr. Yudim's plan. It made Patient Lewis a huge project but she was, after all, a trained nurse, and in it for the long haul.

A BETTING FOOL

I was sitting in the Biblical Sports Book taking bets for Uriah who had gone into Bethlehem to pick up some dates. Uriah had a thing for dates, liked them rolled up with sesame seeds, honey, and sugar, you could only get them at a special joint in Bethlehem.

I hadn't been there five minutes when a tall, dark-haired fellow I never seen before strolled in. He carried himself well and looked to be in good shape but his clothes were another matter. His sandals were paper thin and his robe, though once expensive, was bleached white and frayed around the edges. We saw his kind in the Sports Book all the time, a busted-out prophet or bankrupt camel dealer. He planted himself in the middle of the room and stared at the price lines like he was hypnotized. I waited a proper interval until I decided that if he was gonna get mystical he could do it somewhere else.

"Can I help you?" I said. He turned and looked at me and for the first time I noticed his piercing black eyes.

"Yes," he said. "I'd like to ask about some prices."

"That's what I'm here for, sonny. Ask away." He closed those black eyes, did a little thinking.

"Alright," he said. "I see you have Moses as a big underdog to come down from the Mount with the Ten Commandments."

"100-1," I said, "with ten or any other number of Commandments. See, Moses has started to take himself too serious, overestimate his abilities. The only thing Moses is gonna come down with from the Mount is bunions and less credibility."

"Doesn't Moses claim he'll do it?"

"Yeah, and when my wife asks me why I come home late at night, I claim I'm taking a course at the Rabbinical Annex. Claims don't mean nothin', sonny."

"The man has a reputation for doing what he says," said the stranger. "How many people had him parting the Red Sea at 8-1?"

"Bad comparison. Moses was born in a river, knew all about water. The parting was about his knowledge of sea currents. This commandment thing is a whole new game."

"Perhaps," he said. "But 100-1 is a nice price."

Once again, he closed his eyes as if lost in thought. Then he started swaying and humming. He was a weird one, that was something you could bet on. After a few minutes, he emerged from his trance.

"How about David versus Goliath?" he asked. I checked the line. The guy sure liked longshots.

"60-1," I said. "Against David."

"But David's undefeated!"

"He's fought nobody. You got an unproven lightweight going up against one of the toughest heavyweights in history."

"What about the triumph of Good over Evil?" asked the stranger.

"Son," I said, "betting takes logic. You keep betting Good over Evil and you'll end up mucking out camel stalls." If he wasn't doing it already.

I was gonna point out that if he used more logic and less emotion he might be able to afford a new robe. But I thought better of it. Maybe it was the intensity of those eyes looking at me, through me. Truth be told, the stranger was beginning to make me nervous.

"So, what do you wanna do?" I said. "Wanna make a bet or what?"

For an answer, he reached into his pocket, took out a fistful of shekels, and began counting it fast, like a dealer or croupier at the Adam Club.

"I have 2000 shekels here," he said. "What odds do you have Job at?"

I looked up at the board and found Job versus The Tribulations.

"23-1 against Job," I said. "But I hear God is gonna put the wood to Job. Boils, plague, fire, frogs, you name it. 23-1 might be a short price. Most of the smart money's coming in on God."

"I want 2000 shekels to win on Job," said the stranger.

"Wh-what? All of it on Job?"

"It's the right bet," he said. "Job believes he can do it and that's enough for me."

What could I do with the fool? I took his cash and wrote him out a receipt. He took it and tucked it away in a pocket of that tattered robe. What a degenerate, walking around in a shmatta like that making two grand shekel bets. I noted his bet in the ledger and when I looked up he was halfway out the door.

"Good luck," I called, feeling a bit sorry for him.

"Thanks." He winked one of those black eyes at me. "But I don't need luck. I have faith."

Many sunsets later Eshad, our official scribe, brought us news of

Job's astounding upset victory. Fortunately for us most of the action had been against Job. In fact, the stranger's 2000 shekel bet was the only winning wager. Uriah and I were discussing our favorite oases when the stranger walked in to cash his bet. Uriah took one look and nearly fainted.

"Job," moaned Uriah. "You bet on yourself!"

"Why not," the stranger—Job—smiled. "It seemed like a good thing."

Uriah had no choice but to pay Job off. Nervous that word of Job's coup would get back to the other bookies and make him look like a fool, Uriah made me promise not to tell anyone how he was suckered.

I kept that promise and never told a soul while Uriah was alive. But I'll tell you, it used to amaze me when I heard people talk about the remarkable Job and how his faith prevailed.

See, I always figured what got Job through was that 2000 shekel bet he made on himself.

THE SQUIRREL

He couldn't remember the last time someone had been in his hotel room. He borrowed a vacuum cleaner and ran it over the threadbare carpet for a half hour. It was hard to tell if anything came up. He scrubbed the sink, the shower, the tile on the bathroom floor. He got a couple of fresh towels, the first in several months, and hung them proudly from the racks in the bathroom. Housekeeping gave him a fluffy red bedspread, and he was able to hide a huge grease stain by angling that side toward the wall.

While waiting for her, he tried to watch TV. He couldn't concentrate. He picked his nose until he felt cartilage shift and then started on his ears. Every time he heard a car door slam, he leaned out the window and peered down five stories below.

Six, six-fifteen. In the bathroom mirror he saw a pimple, a large pimple, forming on his neck. It couldn't be, not tonight. With a tweezers and skill of a Civil War field surgeon he worked at it until he had succeeded in creating a bloody lesion the size of a quarter. He had just slapped on a Band Aid when he heard a knock on the door.

He moved to it as if in a trance, opened it. There she was, in her blue parka, blue jeans, and sneakers. She looked so free, so spontaneous, so damn beautiful.

"Hi," he said. "I'm surprised security let you up."

"Security?" she said. "You mean that old guy at the desk who was talking to himself?"

She came in and tossed the parka on a chair He grabbed it and hung it in the closet. She looked around the room.

"Nice place you have here," she said. He wasn't sure if she was being sarcastic.

"It's humble but I call it home. You want a tour?" He showed her the bathroom, pointing out the towels, and the closet. They found themselves standing in the middle of the room.

"How about TV?" he said. "*Jeopardy's* on in five minutes."

She pressed against him, kissed his neck. Her lips moved to his mouth, hands to his crotch. Within minutes they had added several stains to the bedspread.

Afterwards, he wondered if she was hungry or if they should watch TV. She was quiet. The sound of the evening traffic rumbling across 43rd Street banged against the window. He got up to take a piss and heard her call, "When you come out you'd better be hard." After he pissed he rubbed his cock but it didn't work. When he got back in bed he realized she had been kidding. She snuggled next to him and sang him songs in her beautiful, church choir-trained voice. She did some impersonations. Daffy Duck: "Hey, mister, how'd you like to take a duck out to dinner?"

They decided on a tiny Indian restaurant on 45th street that featured great Chicken Vindaloo and the angriest waiters in town. He had never seen anybody else dine there. During dinner a roach the size of ping pong ball crawled up the wall and they laughed and laughed.

The next morning she called him just after he got to the office and told him what a great time she had and that she loved him. It lit him up, he was on fire, a Norse Conqueror, Bernie the Strong. He hit the phones and killed. Client after client buckled beneath his sword of persuasion and signed up for the Cable TV package he pitched. By noon he had drummed up more than $700 in commissions. She called and asked if he had time to have lunch.

They met in Central Park, strolled hand in hand by the lake near 70th street. They got Sabrett hot dogs and sat under an elm. Little squirrels skittered across the lawn, drunk with need to prepare for impending winter.

"You know," she said. "You remind me of a squirrel."

"Why's that?" he asked. His mouth was full of delicious beef juices.

"You make all this money yet you live in a tiny little hole in what amounts to a tree trunk. You forage, forage, forage, sell, sell, sell and accumulate and hole up, waiting. What are you waiting for?"

"I thought you liked my place."

"It's lovely for a room in a welfare hotel. I asked you a question. What are you so afraid of?"

He made kissing noises to one of the squirrels. It got up on its haunches and regarded him with interest. He kissed again. The squirrel hopped toward him and stopped about five feet away. More kissing noises couldn't get it to budge. He threw it a piece of bun. The squirrel picked it up, jammed it into its mouth, and scampered away.

"Isn't that amazing?" he said. "They come when you call. They trust you, like pets."

"Like they're trained," she said.

Two weeks later he waited for her at a jazz club on the Lower East Side. She never showed. She didn't answer the phone at home the next day. He was a basket case at work, stared out at the city, feeling lucky that the glass was thick and strong. He went to her apartment in the afternoon and waited.

She called a week later. She had met somebody and was living with him. She was sorry, it happened, that's just the way it was. He heard himself wish her luck, told her he loved her and that he always would. She thanked him and hung up.

After it fell apart he moved to California. He found a little room in a fleabag hotel on Rampart and got a job delivering balloons. He discovered that the waiters were friendlier in California.

But the squirrels, well, they kept their distance.

THE LOAN

I was at the track the other day with my friends Donnie and Bert. Donnie's a good guy, quiet, the guy can barely get up of the chair to waddle up and place a bet, but I hear he sports a 220 average in his Tuesday night bowling league. I respect good bowlers. Bert is a retired music industry mogul in his eighties, a sweetheart who knows the lyrics to every song ever written, including some he penned in grade school. The problem is that Bert is liable to burst into song at any moment, in a reedy, annoying voice, like when I am close to finding the winner of a horserace. He is also fond of putting his hand on my arm, in a paternal way, as he regales me with stories of his industry days making tons of money and getting lots of pussy. Once again nothing in which I am very interested. But I like Bert, and although his skills as a raconteur could use improving, it's no big deal.

On this particular day, the one-time mogul music producer is in need of a loan. Apparently, some of his horse selections have not run as expected. He tells me of this need while casting dolorous puppy eyes at me. Bert knows I always carry a lot of cash on me. I'm not sure why I do, I don't bet much. I think I simply like the feel of it in my pocket.

"How much, Bert?"

"Eight hundred will do it," says Bert.

That kind of slows me down. I have never lent Bert more than three hundred. I take in Bert's stained shirt and pants. They look like they haven't been washed since Tide came out with a liquid. His fingernails are cracked and dirty. The filthy baseball cap on his head that says Apex Motor Service is coated with cat hairs. Speaking of hairs, Bert hasn't had a shave in a while, and the profusion of wispy gray strands accumulating along his jowls gives him the look of someone whose next dining experience might be at the LA Mission. But Bert has always paid me back. So, I reach into my pocket and with a flourish whip out my stake. I peel off eight Franklins and give them to Bert.

"You're the best," he says. "I'll have it for you Monday."

I say, "No problem."

Monday comes and goes and no Bert. I don't usually go to the races Tuesdays and Wednesdays, but since Bert's phone is going straight to message I travel down to the simulcast theater to see if my eight hundred bucks, I mean my friend, is lurking about. Nope, and no one has seen him, not even Donnie, who I know is telling the truth, because when he's not his huge goiter leaps about like a spawning salmon in a whitecapped river.

So, it is yesterday as I am cashing a small bet on a turf race at Pimlico that I get the grim news from a reliable source. Bert passed away on Monday night, died in his sleep. Now, I have been working on being more loving, what with the twelve steps and all, but at that moment all I thought was: that cocksucker, how am I going to get my eight hundred? I knew it wasn't great form, but later that night I called his wife Wendy to offer my condolences, and also to gently filter in the issue of the outstanding debt. The sound of the phone smashing down sent shock waves through my brain.

Though I haven't been invited, I'm thinking I'll head over to Bert's for the memorial service after the funeral, just to pay my respects.

THE INTERLOPER

The Universe seemed to be mimicking the stages of the relationship. When he first moved into her beach house in San Pedro, the sun would rise every morning, disc-like, framed by a cobalt sky. Now, almost every day fog shrouded the sunrise, and when the sun did finally appear, rather grudgingly, it seemed to drag the gray mass of Catalina Island out of the ocean as if by a magnet.

Things were already tenuous in the relationship before she brought the monkey home. It was a hirsute and spindly thing, no more than three feet tall, and wore a perpetual look of consternation on its grizzled face. In the mornings, lying in her bed overlooking the Pacific under luxurious satin sheets, he would feel like an interloper, incapable of expressing himself, as if truth was an obstacle rather than a conduit to his being. The more she failed to acknowledge his inchoate withdrawal, the more he lost faith in her, perceiving her inability to grasp his shallowness as proof of her own. After she served him a breakfast of fresh sliced mango and toasted English muffin slathered with orange marmalade, his favorite, and left him with a kiss on his bald head, he would gaze over the deck railing at the waves as they cascaded in prismatic bursts upon the shore. Instead of infusing him with hope and screenplay ideas, the algae-laced froth evoked the monotonous implacability of the Universe, a conveyor belt of unoriginal thought, incapable of being comprehended by an unformed savage such as himself.

And sitting there, mocking him through watery brown eyes, was the monkey. She had never said why she had purchased the creature. In the absence of an explanation, the man obsessed about random events responsible for evolutionary upheaval, culminating in the ascent of upright, primordial man, a being capable of incremental cognition, testicular juices spurting upward into a medulla oblongata the size of a raisin. To put it plain, he believed it was her way of saying he was no better than an ape.

From time to time, unable to write, he would rise from the laptop and wander about her home. She would be at the gym or with her many women friends. I love the ladies, she would tell him over and over, as if to remind him of the lesser status of his gender. He found himself rummaging through her papers and drawers, looking under the mattress, garden planters, and bases of standing lamps, seeking an explanation for his existence. It was on one of these clandestine expeditions that he discovered, in an old matchbox featuring a mariachi band on the cover, two tarnished wedding rings. She had never spoken about being married. Were they hers? If not, whose? He perceived it as yet another impediment to renewed intimacy.

He was startled when he became aware of being watched. He thrust the rings into the box and hurled them into a drawer. When he looked up he saw the monkey just three feet away, picking its nose and caressing its testicles. He ran from the creature and back to the deck, slumped on the lounge chair, laptop still unopened, and resolved to leave her. But the sun was warm and comforting and melted away his conviction, leaving in its place a yearning he could not identify which, though calming, made the sleep he craved difficult …

… and yet he must have drifted off, for he was in a dream, a dream where he was bowling while naked… when he was brought to his senses by a tapping on his shoulder. He awoke to see the monkey, and on its hairy index finger was one of the wedding rings. My God! Was she married to the thing? He lurched to his feet and attempted to grab the creature, but with a series of staccato shrieks the monkey bounded to the deck railing and, with unmitigated hubris, taunted him by slowly rotating the ring, wrist over palm, as it was a QVC model.

The man ran across the deck and launched himself at the beast, but the monkey's ancestors had evaded faster predators than a sixty-five-year-old unemployed writer with arthritic knees, and it clambered out of the way. The man went flying over the railing like a missile, executing a tricky double somersault and half-pike before smashing headfirst on the rocks fifty feet below.

The monkey whooped and hollered, unleashed a prodigious turd which it flung against the deck window, then picked up the man's laptop, opened the cover, and powered up.

RISING FORTUNES

I had been rooming with a guy named Stan Stevens for about a year. I met Stan through Tenement Chums, a low-ball roommate agency for people who wanted digs for under $600 a month. We shared a small, one bedroom next to an Exide Battery factory in Vernon. Stan and I had minor differences. I was clean while Stan was the kind of guy who left stained underpants on doorknobs and rarely flushed the toilet. But he paid the rent on time and kept to himself. So it worked.

Around that time, I started dating Phyllis Levine, a self-proclaimed Hollywood producer I met at a Kinko's in Azusa. The fact Phyllis had never produced anything in the ten years since coming to LA didn't stop her from talking up projects that were in Woody's, Martin's, or Quentin's hands. For some reason her unjustified enthusiasm had the effect of cheering me. Our dates consisted of sitting on her sofa, watching the E! Channel, eating from cold cans of Campbell's products with plastic forks, and fucking.

Phyllis had a wet little body. I mean *wet*. Within seconds after our lips met she would become as slippery as a cod. She said the wetness was due to a glandular condition called hyperhidrosis which caused her skin pores to open wide and excrete moisture when she became excited. The only thing I minded was that from time to time Phyllis would slide off the sofa during sex.

One day, while watching an infomercial for a pill called Longitude, a pill guaranteed to add inches to one's penis, I became intrigued and ordered a six-month supply. I mean, Phyllis wasn't complaining but I thought, hey, with an extra few inches I could get better leverage the next time she started body surfing off the sofa. I didn't tell Phyllis about the plan. It seemed best to surprise her. I took one pill each morning with fruit juice. I carried a ruler, measuring myself incessantly, to no avail.

It was about that time that Stan the roommate changed. He did laundry. Mopped. Flushed. Stopped picking his fungus ridden toes during dinner. He claimed he was depressed. That was fine with me. I was hoping he'd sink lower, as the windows needed cleaning and the grimy carpet was begging for a shampooing. I came in one night to find Stan kneeling on the window ledge. As we lived in a basement apartment he wouldn't have done much damage if he jumped. I talked him down with a promise to buy a quart of Lysol.

A couple of nights later I bounced in after driving my Super Shuttle Bus, eager to grab a shave, shower, pop a Longitude pill and go off to see The Princess of Damp. Stan was sprawled on the couch, garbed in underpants, a bottle of Longitude—an empty bottle of Longitude—at his feet.

"I've done it," said Stan. "I'm going to heaven, Jimbo. I ate them all. A hundred pills."

"Jesus, Stan, do you know what you've eaten?"

"Who cares? I figured a hundred of anything would be enough to send me on the final ride."

I dialed 911, although I didn't see the need. With all the good those pills had done I figured they had less value than Pez.

My doubts about Longitude vanished within a half-hour. Accompanied by Stan's horrified moans, we witnessed an incredible transformation. By the time the paramedics arrived they needed two gurneys, one for Stan and one for his engorged member. A male paramedic fainted. A female paramedic proposed.

As for me, I ordered a case of Longitude. I'll keep you posted, so to speak.

GOD'S INSTRUCTIONS TO THE LUSTING MAN

Verily I say unto you, look not lasciviously upon the woman your best friend is dating, for it displeases me. When that woman is introduced, do not permit your fingers to grasp her hand longer than necessary; nor think of the three of you naked in a Jacuzzi; nor imagine sticking your tongue in her mouth; for it gives your Lord on High the creeps.

And your former wife's daughter, now that the young woman is at the age of consent, abandon thoughts such as "we go well together" or "if it's okay for Woody", for such thoughts cause within me the need to lose my breakfast and cause a tsunami in Eurasia.

And while driving, gaze not with lust upon those gorgeous joggers along San Vicente Boulevard; nor, as you watch them imagine how their sweat tastes, lest you anger me and your car somehow swerves into a hydrant, causing an airbag to explode into your fat face, which will smart, trust me.

If you must get a massage, think not the young masseuse cares when she says "I so horny for you, honey", or that her moaning signifies she enjoys you touching her breasts, for to think suchly means you have less sense than a raccoon, and that irks me, as I have created you in my image, although I ask myself often, what was I thinking, as I could have had a V-8.

Divorce yourself of the notion that women in the Spam section of your e-mail want to meet, spank, or marry you, for whilst you would not eat of the Spam, why for do you read of it?

Remove thy profile from dating services in which you describe thyself as athletically built, wealthy, and interested in marriage, for you are chubby, tapped out, and as interested in nuptials as I a game of Yahtzee with Beelzebub.

Forswear staring at asses, especially the servers at the Jamba Juice at Pavilions in West Hollywood, as several belong to young men. While you're at it, get your eyes checked and gaze upward and appreciate the true essence of a woman, her face, her eyes, her soul.

Disabuse yourself of the notion that the waitress who smiles and touches your hand as she takes your order wants you to mount her, for there is a better chance the sky will open and rain kumquats than you shall embrace her; and know too that her recitation of the fish specials does not constitute a vow of eternal love.

And verily, and I say this but oncely, play with yourself if you must but close the blinds, lest you cause passersby to stumble and faint, for who wants to see an old putz working his shaft while watching Sports Center. Certainly not I, who, unfortunately, seeth all.

And, verily, I sayeth unto you: Get Thy Sorry Ass to an AA Meeting.

DATE NIGHT

She let him into the apartment and the first thing he saw were the lace doilies on the dining table and the menorah on the window sill. Items an old Yid would have. Yet he smiled, took her moist hand, and let her guide him to the couch.

For the better part of an hour he listened to her rattle on about her disgust with the teaching profession. When it was his turn to speak, he confided that he sometimes felt out of control, as if he was on a mechanical ride that wouldn't stop. When she asked him to elaborate, he looked at his watch and suggested they watch TV. The Lakers were on. When he left, she gave him a little bag of figs and told him to drive safely. He said he always did and then waited an hour and a half for the bus on Burbank Boulevard.

Before he saw her again, he stopped by a pawn shop that had a huge selection of synthesizers. He wanted jewelry and finally settled on a broach made of deep green jade. It looked like something his grandmother wore, so he thought she'd like it. On the way out, he noticed a large scimitar hanging from a hook on the wall. The blade was long and smooth and looked razor sharp.

She loved the broach. He could tell because later in the evening she arranged some throw pillows on the floor and snuggled with him. They hugged and kissed and she rubbed his crotch, transporting him to a place he had experienced only a few times in the penitentiary. But when he unzipped his fly and attempted to slip his penis into her mouth she became incensed.

"How could you," she fumed, "in this day and age? Why, Magic Johnson has AIDS, you …. you animal!"

Death and sex, sex and death, penis, death, sex, kill, rumbled the voices inside his head. They're ruining it again, he thought, and the pressure built until he thought he'd bust. But then she brought him milk and cookies and he zipped up his fly, munched Oreos, and left with a promise to come for dinner on Saturday night.

Date night.

On Saturday afternoon he browsed the pawn shop again. He couldn't decide whether to buy her a candelabra or a small mandolin. Then the gleam of the scimitar caught his eye.

He went and took it from the wall, felt the purifying steel whipsaw in his hands. It made a soft whooshing sound as he swung it over his head. He paid for it with a crisp fifty-dollar bill and the nervous pawnbroker threw in a rhinestone studded scabbard free of charge.

She greeted him at the door wearing an apron with ducks on it. The house smelled of chicken and onions. She seemed pleased when he gave her the scimitar and said she would mount it over the dresser, the dresser which was a shrine to her parents, and which had hundreds of photographs detailing her life crowding every shelf.

As she was dicing carrots into a steaming pot he came up behind her and cupped his hands over her breasts. She dropped the dicer and turned to face him, mouth open and hungry. As their tongues met the steam from the bubbling soup bathed them in a savory mist. He yanked her onto the counter, sending several sweet potatoes flying into the wall. He threw up her house dress and grabbed at her panties. Her eyes got wide.

"What the hell are you doing? What? What the hell is it? Is that all you can do with your big goddamn penis? Want to put it in me like a donkey?" She pushed him back, scrambled down from the counter, smoothed her dress.

"You don't come into my house when I'm cooking a nice meal and throw me into the food with your big semen-brain," she said. "Not without kissing me first. I could die from your damn sperm, for god's sake."

She turned her back to him and resumed dicing vegetables. "Every day we hear things and there's so many diseases, my god."

His mind was a riot of tribal rhythms and chanting war voices. Death, sex, death, sex, sex, death, evil, penis, touch, die, look, evil, come, omba, omba, ahhhhhhhhhh…

He went to the scimitar and pulled it from the scabbard. She was still talking a mile a minute when he crept up behind her, raised it, and swung with the grace of a home run hitter. It sliced through her neck like butter. Her body took three stutter steps, crashed into the refrigerator, and crumpled to the floor.

But the head. God! It sat on the counter, the mouth still moving, and words were coming out. "I think we have a future," the head was saying, "but. … I want you to … love me." As he watched, fascinated, the words came slower. "A commitment. … is important … is … I need love … please love me …" And then it stopped.

When he was sure she was finished, he picked up the head and stared into the sightless eyes for a while. He arranged the mouth into a pout and tucked the lips around the teeth. He played with her features like a mad embalmer until they suited him.

Then he unzipped his fly, stuck his penis into her mouth, and moved in and out. The warm blood from her neck made a nice lubricant. He guided the head with both hands, back and forth, faster, moving her to his satisfaction. In less than a minute he shot a load deep into her throat.

He nearly fainted from the release. When he recovered, he had a big bowl of her excellent chicken soup, tucked the head under his arm, and went for a stroll on Haskell Avenue.

TWO RABBIS

My catering company was hired to provide a barbeque lunch at the Jewish Museum and my grimy grills had to be sanctified for the occasion. Two rabbis were coming to my warehouse to kosher them. Although Jewish by birth and forced into Jewish slavery until the age of sixteen, I had no idea the koshering process was such a serious business.

The two holy men, dressed in dark suits, white shirts, black hats and black shoes, arrived in a black Kia a few days before the event. We gave them a dolly and they wheeled a large trunk over to the barbeques. For several minutes they hovered about, pointing, muttering "oy vey," and shaking their heads.

They finally opened the trunk. It contained a frightening collection of tools: blowtorch, claw hammer, chisel, bolt cutter and, I kid you not, a gun that one of the rabbis slipped into his waistband.

The rabbis went to work. It was like watching a tire crew work a NASCAR pit stop. A thin metal plate was welded about six inches over the grill tops. Pockets of grease were chiseled away. The blowtorch was run across every inch of surface. Welds were snapped with the bolt cutter. Finally, the rabbi pulled the gun from his waistband.

"The money's in the office!" I yelled. He gave me a curious look, squeezed the trigger, and oil spurted across the grill legs. A piece of thick blue plastic wrap was stretched across the grill tops and adhered to the sides with tape. The utensils were treated as well. Before leaving the rabbis swayed back and forth, murmuring prayers.

"Whatever you do," said one of them, "do not remove the shevotim—the plastic—from the grill. It's a huge sacrilege!" I nodded, we shook hands, and they drove away.

That night as I was about to leave the office, I got a call from a distraught production company on the Fox lot. The caterer hired for a wrap party had the flu. Could my company grill pork ribs and Italian sausages for three hundred guests the following night? For a ridiculous sum of money? I glanced at my plastic wrapped kosher grills. Thought about my huge credit card tab.

"We'll be there," I said.

The next morning my chef and I carefully removed the sacred blue wrap. Getting it back on might be tricky but for the money the

Fox people were offering we'd do it.

We cooked the hell out of those pork ribs and sausages. The beer flowed and the cast had a ball. When we finally rolled into the warehouse at four in the morning we had just enough energy to clean the grills and re-fit the plastic wrap. Except for a small wrinkle or two it was perfect.

Two days later we arrived for the barbeque at the Jewish Museum. The two rabbis watched carefully as we unloaded. As they examined the grills I held my breath. When they finally gave me a thumbs up, I exhaled.

The attendees loved the food. Occasionally someone asked if I was certain the meat and grills were kosher. I assured them they were. For the doubters, the two rabbis came over and backed me up.

That night I crawled into bed for a good night's sleep. The whole koshering business had taken a toll. As I closed my eyes I saw a bearded, kingly figure sitting on a throne and pointing a scepter at me.

"You're some shmuck, thinking you could get away with that stunt. I can forgive cutting Hebrew classes when you were a kid, mocking the cantor, not observing the Sabbath, getting divorced, the drugs, booze, horses, not going to temple on High Holy days, even eating pepperoni pizza on Yom Kippur. But this? This I do not forgive. Do you not have any shame? DO YOU NOT HAVE ANY SHAME? You better make this right, you putz!"

I called the Jewish Museum the following day. They were surprised and gratified at my offer to provide free luncheons throughout the year.

On my kosher barbeques, of course.

DEATH MASTERS

Now that I arrived at Death Masters I still wasn't certain. But as their ad said, "If you're not certain, you've come to the right place." I was led into the Guidance Den, a small room replete with lounge chair, into which I sank, and a desk behind which sat a beautiful woman in a business suit.

"Good morning, Mr. Lewis. Why do you want to die?"

"That's rather abrupt."

"So's death," she said. "You want maybe a tea or coffee?"

"I'd think you'd serve something stronger."

"Like what—hemlock?" she chuckled. "Seriously, what are you willing to blow yourself up for?"

"Wow. Blow myself up." It sounded strange to say out loud.

"Yep. Kablooie. Death Masters promises that you'll take out at least five civilians with the blast. If you fail to do so, the designate of your choice will receive $200,000."

She paused. Studied me.

"Come on, little man. You with the tortured artist face. Want to die for music? Corporate society is corrupting music. Hundred and ten stations playing the same forty songs. Remind people in your personalized Death Masters Video about the failure of corporations to keep music vital. What do you think, music lover?"

"I like music but I don't think I want to die for it."

"How about film? You've got movie watcher's eyes. But you don't go to movies any more. You can't stand to see endless sequels of sequels, car chases, and TV show re-makes. A few pounds of C4 sewn into your tuxedo going pow-boom on the red carpet of a premiere … now there's a statement. They'll get the message. Hell, the surviving executives will be shit-frightened into making good movies. Your pathetic life will have mattered."

She produced a contract. "Cinema death," she said while writing on it. She handed it to me. "Sign there, there and there."

I handed it back. "Sorry. I'm just not sure."

"What's that?"

"That my death will mean something."

She sighed. "I can't tell you what to believe. You walked through that door. You know what we do. You know that in the past six

53

months our clients have taken their own lives and those of over five thousand so-called innocent citizens. Nothing can stop corporations like one dedicated individual."

I wanted to believe. I wanted her fervor to take root. But I was lost in her brown liquid eyes, pert mouth, wavy brown hair. God, she was gorgeous.

"Ah, dear boy, I should have known." She came from behind the desk and sat on my lap.

"You want to die for love," she said, taking my hand and kissing it. "You want to blow yourself into sweet oblivion to remind the world that a man without love is lost, that corporate corruption can be subverted in one act of passion. That sex cannot be eradicated, that it is good and must be embraced, not manufactured with Botox or lobotomized with breast enlargements, or defrauded with erection pills and penile implants. Your death will spark a renewal in a love that sustains and turns our existence into a teardrop of joy." She had my fly open, was manipulating me, touching my balls, kissing my ear.

"Love is all you ever wanted and this sick world wouldn't let you have it," she whispered. "It was you against them the whole time. You weren't good enough, handsome enough, clever enough. Never enough. But now you'll show them. You're going to die for love, big boy."

She rubbed me with one hand and proffered a contract with the other. I remember thinking as I signed that it would be nice to go off at a high school prom.

EARL

You have a kid, you do the best you can, you think you know what you're doing and, well, you just never know.

I had been married to a woman named Muriel for about a year. She was cute in those days, when she was still a blonde and before her ass got bigger than mine. We were at the dessert bar at Sizzler's on Collins Avenue in Miami when she told me she was pregnant.

"I want to be a mother, but I'm not sure, Dave," I heard her saying. "Maybe I'm not ready for motherhood."

Let's see, I thought, I'm holding just over two grand and I know she'll want me to at least help pay for the abortion, what can that cost, maybe a grand? Alright, I'll still have a nice stake, I can deal with that.

"But I'll never know until I try," she went on. "And so, I've decided to have the baby."

Well, that was a whole different story. After six helpings of bread pudding I felt capable of expressing myself without screaming.

"Honey, I'm a gambler, a horseplayer. You know the lifestyle, feast or famine. How am I going to deal with a kid?"

"Maybe get a real job, like a human," she said.

That was quite a change from the sweetheart who used to go with me to Flagler Dog Track and keep me posted on which dog was taking a crap while I studied the past performances. But we were married now and maybe having a kid wasn't such a bad thing. At least there'd be another little me in the world.

"I won't be able to spend too much time with it," I said.

"I'll take care of *our* child," said Muriel. "Don't worry."

My son Earl was born on January 14, 1975, at six in the morning. I won't say the kid was responsible, but I did stay up all night waiting for him to pop out, and that afternoon I got nosed out of a huge trifecta at Hialeah.

The first few years as a father weren't bad because I wasn't around much. I only saw Earl and my wife during the winter when the horses ran at Gulfstream. The rest of the time I followed the ponies around the country, sending Muriel a few hundred whenever I could, sometimes more if I made a score. She never beefed. She had our son, her friends, Chinese food, and evening courses at the local high school to keep her busy.

When I was around, I was a great dad. I enjoyed taking Earl on long walks up Collins Avenue, during which I would convey to him the great truths of life. We were on such an outing when the great calamity occurred.

"Kid, you got to bet to win if you want to have a chance at the races. Think like a winner, like your old man, and you'll have a shot."

"What's a shot, dad?"

"A shot is a chance, which is what most people ain't got, and you got a shot if you bet to win. See, the difference between the win payoff and other payoffs is huge, and in order to make a profit, you got to bet to win."

"What's a profit?"

"Ah, money left over after I take your mom out."

"Where do you go?"

"Sizzler," I said.

"Why Sizzler?"

"It's an all-you-can eat situation," I said. "But never mind that. The main thing in life is to bet to win and make a profit."

"Mom says horseplayers die broke," said Earl.

"She best hope not," I said, "or she'll end up living in a trailer park eating Spam out of a can with a plastic utensil."

I held up my hand. "I know. What's Spam."

After I told him he said, "Mom bets to show. She says show betting is the best way."

"You must have misunderstood her," I said.

"Nope."

"Well, then," I said, "let me put you straight. Show betting is for pussies and pikers, not horse-playin' men such as us. It's like bettin' you'll get hit by a car, you wouldn't want to cash if you won. Now I never want to hear you say the word show again, okay?"

"But mom says betting show means you collect if your horse runs first, second, or third and you won't go a long time without making money like when you lost sixty-seven bets in a row and—"

"Shut up, Earl, just shut up! I don't want to hear that word show again. Ever!"

"Not even if I want to go to the show, dad?"

"NEVER EVER! Say movie, ya little brat!"

His mouth puckered as if he was trying to make a word and his head jerked back and forth. Then he swallowed and blinked his eyes a couple of times. After he'd been quiet for a while I asked if he was OK. He didn't say anything.

"C'mon, Earl, I'm sorry I yelled, c'mon, please, talk to me." He was silent. It would be a while before it sank in that the last word my son would utter for almost six years was 'show'.

After Earl stopped talking, Muriel never trusted me again. Maybe she thought I molested the kid, because one day I saw her reviewing the private parts of a Ken doll with Earl and pointing to me. Hell, I was almost as upset as she was over what happened and maybe more, because Earl had stopped caring about playing the horses. Instead of the *Racing Form* he read books, thick books, which my wife informed me were the classics. Like I never read Damon Runyon.

We took Earl to every doctor in the Yellow Pages and even a veterinarian, for good measure. Couldn't find a thing wrong. One of them had the balls to say maybe Earl had "just decided to stop talking". Well, what would you expect from a guy whose degree said he'd graduated from Sparkling Grapefruit College.

After a while, it sort of leveled off and we escaped into the things that interested us. Earl had his books, my wife her writing, and I, my ponies. About six long years after Earl stopped talking we went to a picnic thrown by the City of Hallandale. It wasn't a bad picnic, except for when some kids attacked a guy dressed in a Superman Outfit. "Kryptonited his ass," I heard one mutter as his mom led him away. Of course, Earl wasn't involved. He sat under a tree, drinking iced tea and reading something called *Gravity's Rainbow*.

When I heard the prize for winning the egg toss was a hundred bucks, I agreed to play with Muriel. I had just gotten an egg when Earl ran up and grabbed my arm. I was surprised. When Earl got into a book he was usually gone.

"What is it, son?"

He stood there tugging on my arm, working his mouth.

"C'mon, Earl, I gotta play the egg toss."

He pointed to the egg and in a quavering voice said, "Sh-show mee ... shshow ... show me ... show ..."

I don't know what I was thinking but all I heard was that damn word "show."

"Show? Show? Still with that show betting talk, Earl? Didn't I tell you never to mention that goddamn word again?" I was wrestling my arm out of his grasp when my wife reached us and took Earl in her arms.

"He spoke," she wailed, "after six years he spoke and you yelled at him and what's wrong with you?"

Everybody was looking at us.

"I didn't do a goddamn thing," I yelled. I threw the egg to the ground but it didn't break. Jesus, I thought, that egg would have won us a hundred bucks.

We hovered over Earl in the months after, waiting for him to utter his next syllable, but he never did. Muriel gained a hundred pounds, stopped shaving, wearing makeup and deodorant or fixing her hair, and started to bear more than a slight resemblance to Haystacks Calhoun. She referred to me as Death Row Davey and told me there'd be no pardon this time around. When I woke up one night to find her sitting by the side of the bed in her wedding gown, holding an electric carving knife, and humming "To Dream the Impossible Dream," I knew it was time to leave.

With my bag packed, I crept into Earl's room and watched him sleeping, my little son, who looked like me and who was destined to be god only knows what because of circumstances beyond my control. I kissed him on the cheek, put the book *Picking Winners*, by Tom Ainslee, next to his pillow, and walked out of his life.

For some reason, I missed them and maybe that's why over the years my luck got worse and worse. When I finally tapped out, I had to get my first real job since college, selling souvenirs in Busch Gardens.

One day, I was trying to convince some tourist from Anchorage to buy a fuzzy orange banner when a good looking kid walked up with a beautiful babe on his arm.

"Hi Dad," the kid said.

"My God ... Earl." I was about to hug him when I noticed his extended hand. He had a powerful grip.

"This is my girlfriend, Emily."

"Pleased to meet you," I said. Her hand was small and smooth, like Muriel's used to be in the old days.

"I see you're talking again," I said.

"Yeah, I started after you left."

The girl looked uncomfortable. Nobody said anything for a while and for a horrible moment I thought Earl had suffered a relapse.

"You know," he said finally, "Mom went to college and she's a writer now, just had a book published."

"She always could write," I said, and was surprised that I meant it.

He took out a wad of cash—looked like all c notes—and pointed to a bag of oranges and a couple of Dolphins t-shirts.

"You want to buy something?" I asked.

"That's why I'm here," he said.

I got the shirts and fruit. The five-pound bag of oranges felt like a sack of concrete.

"On the house," I said. But Earl handed me one of the hundreds.

"Keep the change, Dad."

I stared at the bill. My son was giving me a ninety-dollar tip, putting me in action and I liked the double the next day at Tampa Bay, too, and yet, as I put the c-note in my pocket, I wasn't all that thrilled.

"Why, thanks, son. Paper or plastic?"

"Paper."

I bagged the items and placed them on the counter. He lifted it as though it was a feather.

"You take care, Dad." Emily leaned over and kissed me on the cheek.

"Sure thing."

I waited until their backs were turned to wipe away a tear that had started trickling down my cheek. And then I couldn't resist.

"Say!"

Earl turned around, an inquisitive look on his face.

"Looks like you're doing okay, Earl. If you don't mind my asking, how you making the scratch?"

"Jeez, Dad, I thought you'd have guessed."

He paused and then at once I knew, and it was almost funny, but I had to hear him say it.

"Show bets, Dad," said Earl. "I make show bets."

EGGS

I couldn't get to the track. I had to accompany my girlfriend and her daughter to an Easter Egg Party up the coast in Santa Barbara. A fancy ranch, where I'd feel worse than usual about being broke. God damn Easter Egg Hunt. Well, I didn't have enough money to go to the track anyway.

The trip up the 101 took almost three hours. We finally arrived. It was some joint: forty acres of lush farmland dotted with horse stables, walking rings, training tracks, workers' quarters, and a huge ten-bedroom main house under construction. In a courtyard were arrayed blue, pink, and yellow linen covered round tables with seating for about sixty people under a huge tent. Each table had an ornate centerpiece containing hundreds of candies and flowers. A large buffet snaked along the periphery of the courtyard and a full bar was set up adjacent to the entranceway.

The hostess, Marge Bennett, a studio hotshot like most of the partygoers, came over and air-kissed my girlfriend on each cheek. My girlfriend introduced me. Marge and I shook hands.

"I see you like horses, too," I said. My girlfriend stepped on my foot so hard that I almost screamed.

"Do you ride?" asked Marge.

"Only the Q1O to Hollywood Park," I said.

Marge looked confused. Then she brightened.

"Why don't you get a bite to eat. I understand the honey-baked ham and homemade red potato salad are divine. After lunch, the children will participate in our famous Easter Egg Hunt." She drew us close and continued in a whisper. "There's some serious money hidden in those eggs this year. Mum's the word."

My girlfriend and her daughter raced off to hobnob with the celebs. I got a plate of food and wandered around the grounds for a while, checking out the stables and the sleek steeds whose fishlike faces hung outside the door netting. Then I went up a steep hill to the main house and, on the way back, stopped by a meadow adjacent to a jumping ring.

Specks of pink, green, yellow and blue peeked from under ferns, bushes, and grass blades. The Easter Eggs. I looked down toward the party. From my vantage point I could see most of the guests sitting around the tables.

I dropped to all fours and crawled into the meadow. My ears were alert for any sound. I raced around like a deranged beetle, opening eggs as quickly as I could, removing the contents, and putting the eggs back where I found them. Marge wasn't kidding. Some of those babies had fifty dollar bills in them. I stopped when my pockets were bulging. There was no need to be greedy. Back at the party, my mood improved. I made myself a strawberry shortcake with fresh whipped sweet cream and four or five kinds of berries.

I couldn't wait to get my hands on the *Racing Form*.

A NOTE TO ATHEISTS

For those of you who don't believe in God, try being jolted awake by a pain in your side so severe that your teeth hurt. After several attempts, you struggle into a sitting position repeating the Serenity Prayer over and over, but it's just words, after all this time, and all that work, just words.

You totter to the bathroom and hunch over the toilet, terrified to see what will happen. It's worse than you imagined. A reluctant, thin stream of urine emerges and it is tinged with red, an unfortunate color for urine. The wave of self-pity hits: how did this happen to me, I'm a good guy, why me, and then you recollect the fifty years of abuse you put your body through and you think, well, yeah, I get it.

You wish you had a friend to call but there's nobody. All your life you've nurtured a solitary existence, thinking it romantic, but in these tortured moments you discover you're a few billion light years away from being Jeremiah Johnson.

You slip on a pair of bathing trunks, a t-shirt and flip flops and somehow make it out the door. In the elevator, down to the garage, a neighbor asks how you're doing. You attempt a smile, almost tearing a small muscle in the corner of your mouth.

You manage to lower yourself into the car and put on the emergency flashers. In spite of the fact you are driving nine miles per hour the smallest bump on Third Street sends an arrow of pain shooting up your anus and into your lower back. You finally get to the hospital on the corner of Alvarado and Third and into the waiting room. There's one patient in front of you and he seems comfortable enough, legs crossed, reading the sports section. Fraud, you think, fighting back the urge to smack the newspaper out of his hands, until it dawns on you he might be waiting for a loved one. You fill out endless pages of medical waivers, signing here, there, no doubt giving away your car, dog, spleen, kidneys, corneas, heart, whatever, who cares, you can't take the pain, you must see a doctor.

They finally take you in, you remove your meager clothes, slip on a robe, and are lowered not so gently onto a bed by a fat aide who smells like onion dip. You're not running a fever, your blood pressure is okay, yet the pain in your side has now blossomed to include all your body parts except the few hairs on the top of your head. And there you lie, alone, shaking, and they leave you for what seems like hours, covered by a thin sheet, and it is cold, and you're certain this can't end well.

In glides a young, thin nurse, purple loose fitting smock and pants, green clogs, blond hair pulled back in a ponytail, pink lip gloss, confident, and she asks how you're doing and you gasp, Not good, I pissed blood. And you stare at her and sense something you barely recognize, it's called humanity, and this nurse is the woman you might have married and had children with if only her breath wasn't foul in the morning, or she looked better in flats, or her favorite singer wasn't Neil Diamond, or she didn't use so much teeth while giving head, or her bathroom didn't smell like cat piss, or the worst sin of all, if she was only intelligent enough—and this nurse, this goddess, puts her warm hand on yours and says, You're going to be fine, I'm not going to let anything happen to you, and you believe her, and in her, and as she says these words, in that exact moment, I ask you: how is possible not to believe in God?

FLEZBAR THE ALIEN

It was a Friday night when the alien first visited Jacob. Jacob remembered because he was in bed with the usual Friday night indigestion due to over-eating at the Sabbath meal. His wife, Myrtle, lay on her side of the bed emitting sounds not un-evocative of the mating call of a moose.

"I have come to you from another planet," said the alien. The creature was perched on the corner of the bed and was unremarkable in most aspects, save for an eye-catching foot long genitalia which quite resembled a human penis and which, Jacob observed, appeared to be circumcised.

"And you may call me Flezbar," said the alien.

Flezbar and Jacob chatted for a couple of hours, during which time Jacob told Flezbar everything Flezbar already seemed to know about him, and Flezbar filled him in on his planet. Jacob felt a great ease with the alien. For years, communication with Myrtle, who he loved more as recollection of fond memories rather than the human as she was currently constituted, had dwindled to no more than an occasional grunt. He had so much more in common with the alien, and not for an instant did it occur to Jacob that Flezbar was a product of his imagination, as he had none.

Over the next few visits, conducted at night, the friendship deepened. Jacob confided how his dreams of being a writer were quashed by Myrtle's insistence that he seek his destiny in her father's fur business, and how her resistance to child bearing had filled him with a trenchant regret he had never resolved in his deepest self. Flezbar lent a willing ear and enjoyed the creamed herring Jacob prepared for him, which he slurped through an antenna mounted on the crown of his head.

"Kosher, too," said Jacob. "So you shouldn't worry."

It was on the fifth visit that Flezbar got to the nub of his earthly visitations.

"I have been sent to procreate with a human," said Flezbar. "Our species is dying out—some say too much fried food—and we must determine if an interplanetary union is possible."

Jacob nodded, vaguely thinking it was a good idea, until Flezbar continued.

"And the human candidate the elders of my planet have selected for me is Myrtle, your wife."

"Myrtle?" cried Jacob, his eyes swinging to her dentures floating in a glass of sediment filled water. "But she has no teeth!"

"Not a problem," said Flezbar, stroking his huge member.

All of Jacob's protestations—Myrtle was eight-five, missing a spleen, was bald as a cue ball, and to the best of his knowledge had not had sex for over fifty years—were of no import. She was the one.

"The critical point is that you not breathe a word of my existence to Myrtle or anyone else."

Jacob nodded, a woodenness filling his soul. How could he not share such news? For days afterward, Jacob wandered about in a daze. For over sixty years he had withheld nothing from Myrtle, save for an indiscretion when, in Las Vegas at a furriers' convention, he had sipped some Manischewitz and went bowling on the Sabbath. He was filled with a sense of betrayal. After a week, sleep was impossible. The remaining few hairs on his head fell off as feathers a sick duck.

"Did you eat some bad fish?" Myrtle queried at last, her first words directed at Jacob in over a month. No, Jacob demurred, but finally, able to withstand his deceit no longer, he told Myrtle about Flezbar, the many visitations, and their burgeoning friendship.

"But what you must know, my darling," said Jacob, "is that Flezbar has been sent here from another planet to mate with and impregnate you. You will have Flezbar's child so that he may save his planet."

Myrtle regarded her husband for a couple of moments, put on her robe, went into the bathroom, gripped the sides of the sink and thought: I never dreamed not having children hurt my poor Jacob so much.

After the sacred promise he had made to Flezbar was violated, Jacob felt as if the weight of an entire rib roast had fallen from his shoulders. He turned his attention to the incipient union and wondered if it would be a boy or a girl. He was embarrassed to admit he was more than slightly curious as to how the mating process would take place.

Flezbar never appeared again. After a month of Jacob's ravings, Myrtle took him to a prominent neurologist who remanded Jacob to a sanitarium, where he lived out the rest of his days humming show tunes and waiting, always waiting, for the return of his friend.

BABY

On an afternoon when the sky glistened with hope, they met at a museum. She approached him as he stared into the eyes of Van Gogh's famous self-portrait, the one the tormented artist painted after he lopped off his left ear.

"It's an interesting painting," she said. He turned and saw her and was taken with her beauty.

"I love this painting," he said, "the eyes" …. and he stared into her eyes—bright, liquid pools of blue—and was captivated.

She looked around the nearly empty room.

"I don't think you care about art," she said. "I think you came here to meet a woman."

Caught, he thought.

"And so you have," she said. "Mission accomplished, little boy. I'm hungry. Do you know a good Chinese restaurant?"

It so happened he knew an excellent Chinese restaurant. On the cab ride downtown, they made small talk. By the time they reached the restaurant, he felt like they were old friends. Yet he had the strange sensation of being in a dream, with this exquisite woman a figment of his imagination. He took her to his favorite joint, the Lin Heong.

"What shall I order?" she asked.

"The shrimp with lobster sauce," he replied, taking control. "It's the best in town."

They ordered and within moments the savory shrimp swimming in the black bean-flavored sauce arrived at the table. He watched her eat, wondering how such a thin woman could put food away like a stevedore. He asked her about it.

"Metabolism," she said between mouthfuls. "I've always been thin and beautiful. My afflictions, I accept them."

"I don't think they're afflictions at all," he said.

"Most men don't," she said. Then she paused and stared at her empty plate as if contemplating refilling it. She elected to pick at the shrimps with her fork.

"I find it amazing that we're sitting here," he went on. "It's like a Woody Allen movie, my going to a museum to meet a woman— I heard it was a great place to meet women—meeting you and coming here and you're so beautiful and …"

... and his voice trailed off into the silence that was his sadness ... and then, softly, "And what do you want with me?"

She snared a shrimp on the prongs of her fork and drew it to her lips, licked the sauce off with the tip of her pink tongue.

"You need to be loved," she said. "You need love very, very badly. I must give you the love you need."

Her eyes bored into him as she spoke, his palms were wet. The waiter slapped the check on the table and for once in his life he didn't pick it up immediately and inspect it.

"This love I need," he said, speaking monotonically as if responding to a hypnotist's suggestion. "What kind of love do I need?"

"The love of a woman's body. You need physical love."

He noticed moisture bubbles forming languidly on the outside of his water glass.

"But you have never experienced the kind of love I am going to give you," she continued. "You can't begin to imagine the pleasure .... However, there may be a problem."

Here it comes, he thought. Some disease, some revelation, some cruel blight to nip this bloom of erotica in the bud.

"The problem," she went on, "is that my love may be too much for you. It could be overwhelming."

"I'll chance it," he said.

"Do you think you can handle unconditional love?" she asked. "The love of a mother for her newborn child?"

"And I guess you'll want me to call you mommy," he joshed.

"Not necessarily," she said. "But you will."

She took him home that night and they made love. It was hot and dirty but was hardly as profound as she had described. In fact, as he dressed in the morning, he was wondering what excuse he could give so he could get away to the racetrack.

He emerged from the bathroom and walked into her bedroom. She was lying naked on top of the sheets. What a body, he thought.

"You don't have to worry," she said. "I've been tested for all the diseases."

"Great," he smiled, buttoning his shirt.

"Look at you, all dressed up," she said. "Like you're going someplace."

"You see, my grandmother's very ill," he lied. "Homebound. I have to visit her."

"God," she said, "you're such a project." All he could think about was putting a couple of beers in his belly and getting to the races.

As he was slipping on his shoes, she came up behind him, leaned over and kissed him and there was something in the kiss, her tongue, the urgency of her body that was different from the previous night, and he felt light-headed and his soul did a little dance. He was vaguely aware of being led to the bed and his clothes and fears falling away and …

… then he was inside her and she drew him deeper and then, he became, he was a mountain, a volcano and the lava in the volcano that was him began bubbling and moving up the insides of the volcano walls … and as he moved into her farther, farther still, he saw no end and the lava boiled up the stone cone and was hot and roiled and churned and then BURST over the top and his life poured, spurted, cascaded out of him into her and he lost consciousness and she held him.

He awoke not knowing anything. He could have been anyone, anywhere, anytime, any. He saw it was night, for the black luminous dark of the city nestled against her bedroom window. She came out of the bathroom and when he saw her he felt love well up within him like a giant tear.

"What time is it? And what day?" he asked. She sat on the edge of the bed and played with the belt of her terrycloth bathrobe.

"Useless concerns," she said. She drew a brush through her hair and inspected the nail polish on her left foot.

"This morning," he said tentatively, "I've never experienced anything like that." He was aware of being naked and drew the sheet around him, for he felt shy and young.

"I know," she said. "Are you hungry?"

"Yes."

She drew him to her breast and his lips closed over her rigid nipple. He suckled with eyes closed and not a care in the world. Then she lifted his mouth to her mouth and she was touching his naked body, his skin, his life. As she caressed him he heard a little voice whisper "danger … danger," but it was a powerless, distant entreaty.

And then he seemed to be a shirt being pulled inside out, felt as if his skin was being drawn off and gently tucked about him and his nerves were exposed, and she played them like an instrument. He heard noises of love, wild rushing of passion, whitewater breaking over rocks, and he wriggled, swam through the water into her and he felt small and young and as innocent as the sun and rain and he felt smaller still…

… and she held him tight and whoever he was, whatever he had learned, whatever had defined him imploded, compressing him into the tiniest, purest pulsation of life, and squeezed from him a small sound that issued from the depth of his soul.

"Mommy," she heard him call. "Mommy. Mommy."

~

The golden shaft of morning light sliced across her eyes, waking her. She turned to find his side of the bed empty. He was gone. She smiled and kissed his pillow.

"Baby," she whispered. "Baby."

She got up and collected his clothes. She placed them in a large paper bag. Later, she would throw them in the incinerator. For a few moments, she went through his wallet, looking at the credit cards, license, and other identification which he would never need again. He had vanished. Disappeared from the face of the earth. No one ever saw him again.

Some weeks later she became aware of a swelling in her belly. A week later the doctor corroborated it: she was pregnant. A new life was growing within her. It was *he* who was growing within her, and she was filled with a sensuous, complete joy.

Now, she knew, she could give him all the love he needed.

LUCKY

It is night and the cold of the 3 a.m. wind jet-streaming off the Hudson chills him to the bone. He walks head tucked into his chest and hands thrust into his pockets, down 11th Avenue. Save for an occasional delivery truck, taxicab, or stray cat, he is alone on this stretch of sidewalk. One of the hands in his pocket is knotted into a fist to simulate a gun. This artificial gun is necessary to protect the $200 in his shoe earned from a 12-hour shift in the taxicab. He makes a left on 46th, goes through a wrought iron gate, and into a seedy brownstone. He has lived in this building for seven years. He bounces up the stairs to the fifth floor. As he approaches the door, he takes a house key and the *Racing Form* from his back pocket. When the door opens, he expects to be jumped by his dog Lucky. Lucky is a mutt, half Airedale, half who knows, and they have been together 11 years. But Lucky isn't at the door this evening.

He walks into the kitchen, concerned. He spots Lucky lying near his bowl of water by the stove, looking up at him with the usual excitement, tail wagging, glistening tongue hanging from a grinning mouth. Why is he lying down?

The answer comes when Lucky attempts to approach him. The dog's back legs aren't working. The dog uses his forelegs to drag himself across the floor. He drops to his knees, holds Lucky's head in his hands and strokes it.

"What happened to you, boy? What happened? You're going to be all right, I swear it. You'll be okay."

Lucky looks like he hasn't a care in the world, snuggling his head into his master's lap. As he reaches over the dog to get a beer out of the fridge, he thinks about taking Lucky to a dog hospital. But it's late; is there a place open? The dog seems happy enough, in no pain. And Lucky is old and has had arthritis for years; it comes and goes, hitting without warning and letting up. He glances at the dog. Never like this, though. When he goes into the bathroom, he sees the dog has shit in the corner. He cleans it up and flushes it. When he comes out Lucky looks crestfallen, as if he has done something bad.

"No boy," he says, kissing the dog's head, "you didn't do anything wrong. You're a good boy."

The first couple of beers feel good after the long night of driving the cab. It has been a grueling night behind the wheel, the low point coming when an angry transvestite tries to drag him through the partition and into the back seat when he refuses to take her-him to Bensonhurst.

What a grind of a job. He looks at the pile of bills on the table. The money. Where else can he make two hundred beautiful tax free dollars in one night? He settles into the easy chair, uses the remote to flick on a rerun of *I Love Lucy*, and cracks open the *Racing Form*. He allows himself to be drawn into it, savoring it. First, he reads a column about a racetrack in New Jersey, then an article about a popular trainer. Finally, the main course: the past performances for the next day's races.

When his eye settles on the data that comprises the biographies of the equine contestants, he feels the peace a believer might upon entering a house of worship. The world outside the racing paper ceases to exist. All cares, real or imagined, stop. Time stops. For years, the only way he knows the day, month, or year is by checking it on the front page of the *Racing Form*.

He reads the paper, studying it and digesting it, until the sun comes up. Then, draining his eighth bottle of beer, he takes off his clothes, lets them lie where they fall, and shuffles off to bed. He is very tired but can't sleep. Horses dance in his mind and one horse in particular. A little three-year old filly in the third race. Every time he tries to turn his mind off, he comes back to that horse. She has a lot of speed. Can she overcome the inside post? If the horse on the outside doesn't break she might be able to sprint out to an early lead. The apprentice won't hurt her chances. He is a good young rider, a natural. But people don't know that yet. And the horse has won on the inner dirt course before. Listed at 5-1 in the morning line. Even if the favorite runs first or second that means at least $5 to place. If he gets to the track with $175 and bets it all to place he'll have a stake of over $400.

He tries mantras, phrases, counting sheep, a variety of sleeping positions, and even gets up and reads a few pages of *The Iliad*, a book from college that he can't seem to lose, no matter how hard he tries. The hands on the clock keep moving, mocking him. Eight a.m., nine, nine-fifteen.

He must finally fall asleep because he is awakened by the phone.

"Yeah?" he mumbles.

"Good morning, my man. It's post time."

It is Doc, his race track buddy. He glances at the clock. A couple of minutes before 11.

"I'm tired, Doc." He yawns. He feels great weariness but underneath, a churning excitement.

"The whole world is tired, friend. Only fools sleep."

"Right, Doc."

"You agree with the doctor, smart boy. Now listen. I want to make the double."

"Double's tough, Doc. Too many bad horses."

"The double's a cinch. You like anything today?"

For a second he isn't certain. Then he remembers the little speed filly in the 3rd race. He is reluctant to talk about the horse, part superstition, part not wanting to hear Doc's differing opinion, if he has one.

"It's an interesting card," he says.

"They scraped the track this morning. Sealed it, too."

"Probably going to rain over the weekend."

"Snow, I hear."

"How do you know they scraped the track?"

"You know the sister of that nurse I've been doing in Jackson Heights? She's grooming a colt for Campo."

"No shit."

Now he is as awake as if someone had poured a thimbleful of adrenalin into his eye. A scraped track means the loose topsoil is removed so precipitation won't play havoc with the track. It means that the track will play fast, real fast. No sucking dirt to tire a horse out. The little speed filly will skip across the surface of the hard, scraped track as if gravity doesn't exist.

"Get over to 42nd and 6th in a half hour," says Doc.

"Yeah, maybe."

"I'll have a cab. Northeast corner. Be there." Doc hangs up.

For a moment, he lies back and contemplates the delicious prospect of the day at the racetrack. He sees Lucky as he walks out of the bedroom. The dog has managed to clamber onto the couch and is lying on its side. When the dog sees him, his tail thumps a weak hello on the frayed couch pillows.

"Come here, Luck," he calls, leaning over and smacking his knees. The dog responds by lunging from the couch and crashing to the floor. Using his forelegs, he struggles into a sitting position and drags himself over to his master.

"Jesus, Luck, you're really hurting, aren't you?" He won't have to ask Mrs. Blossom to take the dog out for a walk. No way can the dog go outside. He ladles a bowl of food, puts it down, and watches in concern as the dog sniffs but doesn't eat. He nods as the dog takes a couple of sips of water.

"Tonight, Luck. I'll take you to the vet tonight."

He feels a momentary tugging. Maybe he should take the dog to the vet right now. But no. The vet would charge a fortune. After he wins at the track, he'll have plenty of money to do the thing right. Buy medicines, get the dog a shot. What the dog needs now is to relax. He shaves, showers, chugs two beers and dresses in six minutes. On the way out of the apartment he grabs the *Racing Form* and gives the dog a hug.

For a while it is the kind of day about which horseplayers dream. Doc has the double good and is ahead almost three grand. The speed filly in the third race outbreaks the field and wins by six easy lengths and he gets back $600 for his $180 place bet. He doesn't lose a bet until the sixth race when his stake hovers around $1,500 and then only a small $50 wager on a first-time starter. After the race Doc, who is still a grand to the good, leaves to get to the hospital.

The small $50 loss starts the slide. He loses $400 in the 7th on a horse he hated the night before and $500 more in the eighth, an unplayable race. He bets his last $478 to place on a favorite in the ninth race, a mortal lock. Or at least that's the way it seems at the time, four hours and 24 beers after he and Doc had entered the track full of hope and confidence.

The horse stumbles badly at the start and the saddle slips. The jockey has no real control and from a distance appears to be riding bareback. Under his own power the horse manages to charge up and challenge the leaders going into the far turn. But the jockey can't steer him and the horse bolts to the outside and loses all chance. The mortal lock, the horse that could not lose, finishes last.

He is dead broke except for a token he is amazed to discover in his pocket. On the train home, the remorse kicks in. What is he doing?

His dog who he loves more than anything is sick. He needs to go to the vet. What the fuck is he thinking? He really fucked up this time. Lucky better be okay. I'd rather die than you. I'm sorry, Lucky, and the rumbling of the train lulls him to sleep and he sees a puppy running to greet him, a little ball of fur, of innocence, of light, full of hope, and trust.

He sprints home from the subway, takes the stairs three at a time, throws open the door of the apartment. Lucky has apparently tried to get into the bathroom. Why, who can know. His still body lies half on the threadbare carpeting, half on the cracked bathroom tile. The dog's body is already skewed in the sharp, rigid lines of rigor mortis. He runs to the dog, kneels beside it. His lower lip quivers and he makes a braying sound as he cries.

That night, around 10 o'clock, he wraps Lucky in a blanket and walks three miles across town to the ASPCA. As if in a daze, he gives the woman a check for $30 which he knows is worthless. He walks home, stopping into a deli to shoplift a pepperoni stick and a box of Pepperidge Farm Cookies. He feels violent and imagines that if anyone comes near him he will attack them. But people leave him alone, as they always do, and he gets home cold, tired, and numb from the day's events. He sleeps like a corpse until the phone rings.

"A new day dawns," says Doc.

"What?"

"Time to get your ass in gear, boy. We've got races to bet." A vague memory of the previous night encroaches.

"I can't, Doc."

"You sound ill. Need a doctor?"

"It's been a fucked night."

"Let me guess. You bet the favorite in the ninth."

"Worse than that."

"What could be worse than that?"

"I don't want to go into it."

His chest is tight. He glances out the window and sees snow flurries drifting from a gray sky. Where is Lucky now, he wonders?

"Are they going to race today?"

"They always race," says Doc. "You need some cash?"

"No man. Not today."

He feels his heart pump the first drop of blood of the day. The lure of the world is greater than the bed. Cobwebs clear as if driven by a storm blast. Lucky is gone his dog is gone his dog is …

"How much?" he asks Doc. "How much can you loan me?"

JUST DESSERT

–A Woman's Story

He responded to my ad. "Full figured 64-year-old fun lover seeks fun loving mate." I used a recent photo. I wasn't trying to fool anyone. He was a fat, 61-year-old retired textile salesman. We met at Coffee Bean. He paid.

As we sat there talking, I saw his eyes staring at my breasts. They are far and away my best feature. Natural C's which have defied gravity. I had on a low cut, tight blouse. He was charming. He listened when I talked. He had a good sense of humor. I knew what he wanted. That was fine. Because that's what I wanted, too.

I had not been with a man in many years. My previous lovers died. I intended to get another one but never did. I touched myself for a while but stopped when it was too much effort.

On our second date, we went to Sizzler since I had a two-for-one coupon. We sat in the back. I had a ball. Once again, he insisted on paying.

I invited him to my house for our next date. I spent hours on the treadmill and lost four pounds. I wondered if he would notice. I made my special beef stew. He arrived with a bouquet of daisies, the sticker said: $6/Ralph's. It took me five minutes to get the grime off my pretty purple vase.

He had good manners. He kept one hand on his lap. He dabbed his mouth with my fine linen and said he had never had such a great meal.

"The secret is sautéing the beef before broiling," I said.

"What kind of sauce?" he said.

"If I told you I'd have to kill you."

We laughed and took our brandies into the living room. I turned on the electric fireplace. He was rubbing my neck and playing with my hair. I hoped he wouldn't be disturbed by the wart behind my left ear. He was kissing me. I was opening my mouth like a teenager. His tongue was inside, maybe a little too far. I put my hand on his crotch. He had a big winky dinky. I was afraid he would be too filled with stew but I guess not.

He reached under my muumuu. I spread my legs. He rubbed the outside of my panties. There was feeling there. Soon we went to the pitch black bedroom. He put his mouth on me for a long time. Then he was inside and it was good. Before he came he withdrew and touched and kissed me until I had an orgasm. There is a god. Then I sucked him until he came. We lay in bed for a few minutes. I could feel him withdrawing. Ten minutes later he kissed me and left.

The next few times he ate without looking at me. After dinner he would push my face onto his crotch and have me suck him. After he left, I would do the dishes wondering when he would cross the line. Just to be ready, I made my special dessert.

One night he said, "You know, I wouldn't mind fucking you but your cunt smells like shit. Maybe you want to get it checked out."

The clock on the mantelpiece read 9:14 p.m. The flickering fire cast spider web patterns on the sofa. I felt naked in my nightgown. In my hand, I had a tissue into which I had spit his come and it felt like fifty pounds. The smell of chicken parmesan lingered; a tear filled me and I felt very small.

"That sauce I use for the beef stew," I said. "The one you asked about? It's a simple beef stock but the secret is molasses, thyme and vinegar."

"Who gives a fuck?" he said.

"I wanted you to know. Anyway, I have a special dessert for you. Wait here while I get it."

KINDRED SPIRITS

We met on OK Cupid. She didn't know it but I fell in love with her during our first phone conversation. I could tell she was struggling, flighty, smart, creative, a bit bonkers and had a yearning for something new and different, as did I. It wouldn't have mattered what she looked like. I knew I had found a kindred spirit. Of course, considering who I was, meeting a kindred spirit might not be the greatest move ever. But such is the way of moths drawn to flame. Sometimes there is no choice.

And so, a scant month after we met, during which time we became inseparable, we found ourselves driving up a winding narrow road somewhere in north Topanga Canyon. There was barely room for my Land Rover and I wondered what would happen if another car came hurtling toward us. Against my will, my eyes were drawn to the steep drop on either side of the road, unprotected by guard rails.

"I've been thinking," she said. She put her hand on mine. As always, I melted at her touch.

"We're doing pretty well, aren't we?"

"Why, sure, angel," I said, "we're doing good. Why, here we are, taking a drive on a Sunday, we've got sandwiches and those $4 fruit juices and rattlesnake anti-venom and a blanket and we're going to have us a fine old picnic."

She nodded and said, "It's just that I think we have to crash and burn in order to grow."

I was thinking, no problem, we'll get there in a few months. It was in our DNA, people like us moved toward what we could never have because we knew, in our hearts, that we didn't deserve it.

"Things are good," I said. "Why don't we enjoy the day?"

It was about her sweet kisses and the lovemaking, the first I'd enjoyed in years, and the thrill of waking up next to another human being, a blessing I had begun to believe was reserved for others.

"Why delay the inevitable," she said, "when demise hastens growth?"

I assumed by crash and burn she meant separate for a while and reach a point where we could build on what was true and real and not be driven by instinctual infatuation.

"I love you," she said, grabbing the wheel and yanking it to the right.

As the car skidded off the side of the road and lofted into the air I felt a curious calm. Her hand was on mine. I noticed how slender and strong it was, the hand of an artist. The ring on her index finger glistened with a small, green stone, a ring given to her by her ailing father whom she adored. Her eyes were shining with hope. Shrubs were banging against the car, the car rolling end over end. I always liked the yellow sundress she was wearing. She claimed it made her look heavy but she was too hard on herself. I adored every bit of her.

"I love you, too," I whispered as the car slammed into a rock and burst into flames. I was thinking that it would have been nice to have the picnic before all this growing took place.

ONE LAST REQUEST

She was lying on the hospital bed, frail, lips chapped, eyes fading.

"Grandson," she said, reaching for my hand with a parchment claw. "You must honor an old woman's last request."

"Anything, Grandma, anything."

"Get me a glass of water."

Now that was easy, even I could handle that. I brought it to her and poured some into her mouth. A little too much went down and she choked. I lifted her head and tapped her shoulders. A small chunk of the flounder she had for dinner popped out, along with a thin stream of fluid.

"Now," she wheezed, "I'll give you my last request."

"But I thought …."

"Don't but me, you nearly killed me, you oaf."

"I'm sorry, Grandma."

"You certainly are. Anyway get me … for my last request … you must … please … please, grandson … I have a yearning for … a piece of blackberry pie."

"That's it?"

"A piece of blackberry pie. Then, I have an appointment with God."

"Yes, sweetheart." I kissed her forehead and ran from the room. God, this was easy, a frigging piece of pie. Even I couldn't screw this up.

I drove to Marie Callender's. "One piece of blackberry pie," I said.

"Blueberry, boysenberry, strawberry, cherry," intoned the bored waitress.

"No blackberry?"

"Blueberry, boysenberry, strawberry, cherry."

I thought about asking her again to see if her head would explode. Then I contemplated getting blueberry. In her weakened state would Grandma know the difference? The mortifying thought of trying to trick grandma on her deathbed sent me speeding down Wilshire to Denny's. No luck. On to Carrow's, Ralph's, Whole Foods, Sprouts, IHOP, a diner on Sunset, Spires, Johnny Rockets, and then, the bastion of baked goods, House of Pies on Vermont. It was at House of Pies that a knowledgeable host confided that blackberries were in season in August. Not great news considering this was February.

"Is there a berry that someone might think is a blackberry?"

"Not really," spewed the font of pie wisdom. "The blackberry has a richness of color and flavor that no other berry, not even the gooseberry, approaches."

It was with great sorrow that I purchased a blueberry pie at Ralph's, a bottle of brown food dye at Smart and Final, and set about preparing the cinematic version of Grandma's last request. When I finished, I had a pie with a black-splotched crust and a gray interior. I was out of options, time and ideas. What Grandma suspected was confirmed: I was a hopeless fool.

I trudged into the hospital and made my way to Grandma's room. I opened the door to discover two nurses stripping the bed.

"I'm so sorry," said one. "Your grandmother passed peacefully in her sleep."

One nurse left the room. The other held my head against her chest and patted me like a dog. Her counterpart returned a couple of minutes later with a cup of coffee and a piece of pie.

"What kind of pie is it?" I asked.

"Blackberry," said the nurse. "It was your grandmother's favorite."

LOVE BITE

I fall off the wagon every few months. I get sober until my hatred for the tame life exceeds my desire not to drink. Then I drink until the situation gets bad enough and I go back and work the steps. Until this last drunk.

I didn't even feel like drinking. I was at the track and just glanced at the bar. A tall, black bartender with an eye patch stood checking out the nearly empty Thursday afternoon grandstand. He looked bored. As if he needed a customer. I stepped up and ordered a Bud. I tell you, that first sip was lip-smacking good. Within minutes I had a whole new outlook. After four beers, I uncovered a great bet in the eighth race. I plunked down my last $6. The horse won like a champ and paid $76. I had cash in my pocket and a headful of beer.

I drove off and bought a six pack of St. Pauli Girl at a liquor store on Century Boulevard. I polished it off on the way to the night's quarter horse races at Los Alamitos. I must have had fifteen beers in me when I hit a $1,200 trifecta in the seventh race. With a pocketful of dough, I drove away feeling better than a man had a right to. It made little difference that I was driving on the wrong side of Bloomfield Avenue.

The beer had made me lucky. Now it made me fearless. With inhibitions in the deep-freeze, I drove north into LA. I found myself driving east on Hollywood Boulevard, leering at babes and wiggling my tongue at muchachas in Civics and Neons. It was a miracle I didn't get shot. I parked in a handicapped zone—after all, I was the best damned handicapper in Hollywood—and wandered into a place called Florentine Gardens.

The joint was packed with beautiful babes and swarthy Latino males gyrating to thump music. Normally I would be as welcome in a place like this as a pope in a nudist colony. But with a big Alfred E. Neuman grin and a what-me-worry attitude nobody bothered me.

I talked with a pretty woman at the bar, about what I have no recollection. I remember taking my stake out of my pocket, waving it around, and offering to take her to Vegas. As we drank, the strobe lights played on her face and her lip gloss danced in my eyes. There was red polish on her long nails. She wore a skintight, black dress. Her jet-black hair was cut short. After ten minutes I was pretty much in love.

As I was blabbing away, she got up and started moving to a disco song, swaying like a reed in a breeze. I experienced a warmth, a sensuousness unlike any other. Maybe she had put something in my drink, I felt drugged. Who cared. I danced with her, she insinuated herself into me. I vaguely remember leaving the club. The air was cool and crisp …

… and suddenly I was raked with nails, mouths opened, I was bitten and I held on and tore at her, legs were opening and she spat and urged and fought and pulled me closer and spread her legs wider, wanting, wet, pulsating, and she was on all fours and I entered from behind and thrust away and at the moment of release she leaned back and lunged and I felt the need to penetrate to the fiber of my being….

. . . and I woke up in an alley. My first thought was my money. I thrust my hands into my pockets. My stake was intact, almost $1,500 bucks! I was overjoyed until realized I was covered with bruises and scratch marks. There was a large puddle of dried blood where I had lain. I couldn't account for my presence in the alley.

My car had been towed. I took the Sunset Boulevard bus to Doheny and walked south a mile or so to my apartment. As I undressed, I noticed a Florentine Gardens matchbook with the name Mikey and the number 310 652 8328 scrawled on the inside cover. I had a flashback of a willowy figure and a carnal rush of seismic proportions. I took the hottest shower of all time and tumbled into bed.

Two days later I was in back in an AA meeting warning of the perils of drinking. Since my epic triumphs at Hollywood and Los Al, I had torn through my winnings, $400 life savings, four cases of Bud, a gram of coke, and my job bussing tables at the Airport Crowne Plaza. I hadn't hit the bottom, I had fallen through it.

I felt good after the meeting. I had what it took to do the deal. I'd get a sponsor and do up a fine program. The key was to embrace the ordinariness of sobriety. No matter how it beckoned, I'd resist the call of the wild. The next morning I could barely move. I tried to walk but the more I moved the worse it was. As the day went on I experienced a prodigious thirst. I drank bottle after bottle of orange Gatorade with no relief.

By early evening I was so stiff I could barely make a fist. A worried AA acquaintance lent me his Kaiser card and drove me to the emergency room on Vermont. A pulmonary specialist saw me right away. He took one look, left, and returned seconds later with an older doc. They asked me a couple of lifestyle questions. I accentuated the sober moments. They took some blood and gave me a shot. Said it might be a good idea if I spent the night. I knew it was bad. You had to have a baby hanging out of your snatch or a tumor swinging from your dome to be admitted to Kaiser.

They asked if I had a dog. Been bitten by a dog. A squirrel. I honestly answered no, feeling increasing dread. I didn't tell them about the alley or the blood or my fear that a pack of rats must have gnawed at me as I slept off the beer and whatever else I had ingested in goddamn Florentine Gardens.

The rabies shots weren't as bad as they say. Two weeks and four shots to my midsection later I was good as new, going to AA meetings every day.

About a month later the close call with rabies was a distant memory. I was getting restless. My sponsor hadn't returned my calls for a couple of days. No one acknowledged me in meetings. I craved unobtainable pussy. While buying a Coke at a 7-11, I found myself staring at the neat rows of beers. The whisper of the wild was becoming a louder voice.

One night I was on my patio getting ready to light up a cigar. I went in to find a match and there, under an old *Racing Form*, was the Florentine Gardens matchbook. When I opened the cover, I saw Mikey's phone number. The top of my head started sweating.

I punched in the numbers. A woman answered.

"Mikey?" I croaked.

"Very funny."

"No seriously, is this Mikey?"

"Do I know you?" she asked.

"I don't know. I think so."

"From where?"

"Florentine Gardens."

"The club?"

"I think so, I can't be sure."

"I've never been there," she said.

"Never there …"

"I don't go to clubs."

"Well…" I paused, feeling like a fool but feeling a weird connection nevertheless. "I don't know, there must be a mistake."

"Maybe," she said.

"Maybe?"

"Because I know a Mikey." I felt blood rush from my feet to my head like an elevator with no springs, no stop mechanism.

"You do."

"Yes."

"How do …"

"Mikey's my friend. Do you want to come over?"

"Why?"

"To meet her."

There was no going back, there never was. The dark, erotic side, that which sustained and killed and which was my ecstasy and my death, was again on the itinerary.

"When?"

"Come now. It's 10226 Pico, near Sawtelle. Ring code 09."

The address wasn't far from my apartment. As my car was still in impound, I rode my bike, careful to keep to the side streets. When I got to Prosser, I went south to Pico and a couple of blocks west to her place. She answered on the first ring.

"Come up the stairs," said a voice through a crackling intercom. "I'll have the door open."

It was a modern building, poorly built. I could hear TVs clearly through several doors. I took the steps three at a time.

The woman at the door: short, stout and matronly. My expectations drained as if I had been gut-punched. Where her left ear had been was nothing but a mound of flesh.

"Hi," she said, holding out a hand missing three fingers. "I'm Stacy. Come on in." I stepped into the sparsely furnished apartment and heard the door lock click behind me.

"You want a drink?" she asked. At that moment sobriety was an elderly uncle who had nothing to offer but regret and a life spent missing the point.

"You got a beer?" I said. She went and got me a cold Foster's. Big Blue. We sat in silence and drank.

"She's in the other room," Stacy finally said. "Waiting for you."

I moved through a row of beads which formed a doorway into a dark room. There was a stink of disease and old sex and degeneracy. A soft keening pierced the air. As my eyes became accustomed to the sparse light I saw the outline of a creature chained in the corner—emaciated, mouth encrusted with foam, straining towards me. Its huge dark eyes were filled with pain and need and I connected with it and felt a wellspring of love and empathy.

And as I moved closer, I could make out the full lips and well-defined ears of a human, but the creature seemed to sitting on haunches. A wet pink tongue whipped across desiccated lips, inviting me. I was filled with dread and desire and a longing to throw myself over the abyss finally and forever.

I drained the Fosters and thought about the dreams I'd had and the rotten bunch of crap it had all become and about the fine moments God had granted me and how impulse had made each a mockery and a last chance as well.

"Go to Mikey," I heard Stacy say. "Go to her and fuck her."

And I did.

HER

It is one of those rare Sundays when I decide to drive during the day. I pick the cab up at my midtown garage as the first orange blaze of light pierces the October sky. I get cab number 607, a peppy little vehicle with a fast meter.

It's hard to say what you'll pick up at 5 o'clock on a Sunday morning. It can be a well-heeled gent going to Kennedy or flotsam floating from an all-night squeeze bar. It doesn't matter because I have cabbie radar and I can smell weirdness a mile away. Most times, anyway.

It is about 5:50 am. I am drifting down Second Avenue. My attention is snagged by a blond in a black leather jacket, skin tight jeans, and black boots running out of the Two Cents Plain at St. Marks and Second. I pull over and she opens the back door.

"Will you go to Brooklyn?"

"Sure," I say. As cute as she is, I will go a lot further.

We are down around Delancey when she opens her jacket and I see pert breasts straining against her tight pink sweater. I say, "I don't usually drive days, but I thought, hey, today, what the hell."

"What's wrong with days?" Her voice is husky and not much louder than a whisper.

"Too much traffic. But Sunday it's not too bad. And I know how to play the airports."

"Play them?"

"You know, when to show up to get a fare."

"How long have you been driving a cab?"

"A couple of years. I'm a writer. You know, trying to write the Great American novel. Driving a cab gives me the freedom to pursue my career as an artist."

She leans forward and puts her long, slender fingers on the open partition.

"I love reading. Have you written anything I might have read?"

"Not yet," I smile. "But I'm trying."

Her name is Angelina. We are chatting away about her work as a beautician and my writerly ideas when we roll up to her apartment in Bay Ridge. The tab is $12.50 and she gives me a $20.

"Keep it," she says.

"No way, Angelina. This ride is on the house." It's the first time I ever say these words.

"Please," she says, trying to force the money into my hand. I refuse.

"Alright then," she says. "Can I at least make you breakfast?"

"Now you're talking," I say.

Her fifth-floor pad faces the water. I can see the Verrazano Narrows Bridge in the distance. It is a modern apartment with bright white carpeting, steel lamps, and black and white couches. I go out to the balcony while she freshens up. When she comes out she is wearing a pair of grey sweat pants and a black halter. Her stomach is as flat as a board, her shoulders wide and toned.

"Scrambled eggs, toast, and bacon okay?"

"Perfect," I say. "Perfect."

And it is. Although I'm guilty about taking time off from work, this is worth it. I am in a class apartment with a beautiful lady who is making me breakfast. I almost have to pinch myself.

Breakfast is ready in a flash. A table in a small dining room is set with placemats, linen napkins and real tableware. The coffee is sure and strong. She slides the bacon and eggs out of the frying pan onto my plate. The rye toast appears dripping with butter. I have never had a greasier meal. Ever. I mean, I love grease. I'll suck a French fry dry as soon as look at it. But this meal out-greases even me. A paper towel hasn't come within ten yards of the bacon. But I chomp it all down, praising her cooking all the way. After breakfast, we go out on the balcony and put away several more cups of her good coffee.

"I grew up close by," she says, "in Bensonhurst. Take the F-train to 18th Avenue, walk two blocks north, that's me. Very Jewish neighborhood. You're Jewish, aren't you?"

"Yeah."

"I love Jewish boys, so sensitive and smart."

"How'd you get into the beauty biz?" I ask.

"I always had a poetic soul, like you. Except my writing, honey, it was, like, roses are red, violets are blue crap. I wanted to express myself, but how?"

"I give up."

"I always loved people watching, honey, people turn me on. I get the idea that since I can't write a story maybe I can write someone else's story—the story their face tells."

"How do you do that?"

"With makeup. I've always been good with the stuff. When I was a kid I would rather put on Mommy's makeup than anything. I know women and I know makeup and I know how to let women tell their stories with it. It's how I express myself. What do you think, sweetie, do you think I'm nuts?"

"Does it pay okay?"

"I have so many regulars you wouldn't believe it. They call me an artiste. Isn't that something?"

"Yeah."

"May I ask you something personal?"

"Sure."

"Are you married?"

I am about to answer when the phone rings. She ignores the first ten rings, then excuses herself and goes into the living room. She speaks softly. After a minute her voice gets louder. I hear the word police. She slams the receiver down and comes back.

"I'm sorry," she says. "Sometimes people just don't get that you have to move on. I'm tired. Will you take a nap with me?"

She takes my hand and leads me into a tiny bedroom that features a twin-size bed and a small chest of drawers with about fifty votive candles on top. She slides onto the wall side on her back and I lie down next to her. Neither one of us makes a move. At some point, she turns and nuzzles against me.

"Just hold me," she says. I put my arms around her. She feels strong. I occasionally kiss her neck. I work my way over to her mouth.

Maybe it is the grease working through me or my guilt about taking the day off or the smell of onions on her breath. Whatever, there is as much passion in that room as my cab garage.

"I really like you," she says.

"Me too," I say. And it's true. I'm not crazy about getting to Bay Ridge but I think we might spend some good times. I kiss her on the cheek and sit up.

"I got to get going. My garage will know something's up if I come in with ten bucks on the meter."

"Do you drive Wednesdays?"

"No."

"Can you come for dinner?"

"Sure, I'd love to." We hug, she guides me to the door, and I am on my way.

By the time I am back behind the wheel, the only things I remember are her tight body and cool apartment. When I reach Manhattan, I am looking forward to our date on Wednesday night as if she is my soul mate.

I can't sleep Tuesday night. On Wednesday to calm my nerves I drink a six-pack or two. I get to Bay Ridge two hours before our six o'clock date. I buy a bottle of Korbel Brut at a little liquor store a block from her place. She buzzes me up on the first ring. When she opens the door, I hand her the champagne.

"What a sweetie pie," she says. "It's the good stuff." She kisses me on the lips and leads me into the apartment.

She is wearing tight jeans and a green halter top and it looks like her friends in the salon have worked on her most of the day. She is glowing and her hair has been teased to blond perfection. She guides me into the living room. We sit on the couch.

"How is the novel going, sweetie," she asks. My first thought is: what novel?

"Oh good," I say, trying not to slur my words. "My hero is a semi-pro baseball player in the merchant marine. He's just sailed from Africa for the Far East. He's gonna play in the Japanese Leagues, be a big star. When the first draft is ready you'll be the first to see it."

She leans toward me, gives me a hug, and puts her tongue in my ear. I tilt her face to mine and kiss her. Her mouth opens and our tongues intertwine. I put my hand on her right breast and play with the erect nipple. She moans and kisses me harder. My hand strays down but she clamps the high school vice grip on it.

"No," she says. "Don't do that."

I figure she wants to serve dinner first. That's fine. I've been drinking all day and man do I have to take a leak.

"I'll be right back," I say. "Just going to the bathroom." She nods and leans back, a vacant expression on her face.

I must piss for fifteen minutes. No camel ever takes a longer whiz. After I finish I scout around looking for a random jar of Percodan or Seconal. There is nothing but toiletries in the cabinet over the sink. I spot a larger medicine chest over a laundry hamper behind me and open it. I get a shock. There are more bottles in that cabinet than in the Port Authority Walgreen's. There is hormone this, hormone that, enzyme this, metabolic that, hormones, hormones, hormones. For a second I can't make any sense of it.

Then it hits me. Her big hands, husky whispery voice, broad shoulders, physical strength, love of cosmetics, sense of sadness, unwillingness to let me touch her. I emerge from the bathroom not knowing what to say or do. She is slumped on the couch, it looks like she is melting. The top of her head is almost on a seat cushion.

"You saw them, didn't you," she says.

"Saw what?"

"I take them, all of them. I have to and I have been for almost a year. I'm going for the operation in two months. Then you can touch me all you like."

"Sweet Jesus."

"Please," she says, "I like you. You're the first heterosexual man I've ever wanted. Please don't make this painful."

"I gotta be going."

"Oh baby," she says and comes to me. She reaches down and grabs my cock.

"It's okay," she says. "I'll have a vagina soon."

I jump back.

"I don't go that way, Angelina. Sorry."

"It's all me, the same soul, don't you get it? Don't you?" Her whispering is now a strident male voice. "Don't be a fool. I'm good for you. I can feel your poetic soul, I felt it from the first moment in the cab. Please."

"That's okay, you take it easy," I say backing away. I sprint down the hall. For days afterward, I'm nauseated whenever I think of that evening.

But it's funny how life goes. As the years pass I find I have frequent fond thoughts of Angelina. I wonder how she is doing, what she looks like. When I take a fare to Brooklyn I make it a point to drive by her building, hoping to see her. But I never do.

And I always, always, think of her … as her.

THE CAT

I was sitting in my house feeling like Hitler must have while waiting for the end in his bunker circa 1944. My mind was producing an ominous stream of morbid thoughts and dark fantasies. My wife, whom I considered to be the source of my black mood, was at the massage parlor blowing and fucking enough men to support me in grand style. She did this because she loved me. I, on the other hand, pretended to love her.

In fact, the more time I spent with her, the more I loathed myself for selling my soul for that tainted whorehouse money. At night when she coerced me into sex and I became the eighth or ninth man to enter her wet, stinking hole that day, my disgust grew until it enveloped me. Sad to say, my greed was stronger than my disgust, and fortified with a wide variety of pharmaceuticals, I plunged away, gradually losing myself in the dark forests of human malevolence.

On this particular afternoon, I was especially annoyed, for she had hidden the drugs again. Her depriving me of the one thing that gave me hope was becoming a real issue. She would dole the Quaaludes out to me at night, attempting to control me and prime me for sex. I let my mind dwell on the high platform heels she wore to offset her dwarf-like stature; the stinky flesh-colored cream she used to cover the whiteheads at the sides of her mouth and chin; her love of that terminally boring game, cribbage, which she forced me to play, and, worse, expected me to lose at, every night; and her four-hour daily diet of soap operas which I had to tape and which she watched in the evenings while puffing on vile smelling clove cigarettes.

These thoughts set my guts kicking and I felt a tic over my left eye start doing a dance. For a while I submerged myself in a Steven Segal movie and a quart of chocolate pudding. But when I got up and strolled through the apartment eyeing further evidence of her—the witch's altar in the corner of our bedroom complete with animal hooves, hair, and amulets; stockings and stained panties thrown over chairs; and an infinite number of hair-matted brushes and encrusted cosmetic bottles—I was thrust even further into the pit of rage and despair.

I was alone in the apartment except for the cat. Her cat. A fat orange Persian who resembled one of those furry things Russian women stick their hands into so they don't get cold. As cats went, he wasn't a bad sort, except for two flaws: he was totally in love with and dedicated to my wife. You can understand why I hated this cat, can't you? Certainly, anyone who liked that bitch was no friend of mine.

I called to him but he ignored me. On one level, I didn't blame him. God only knew what I did to him when I was stoned. Yet his disdain had the effect of focusing my rage and it occurred to me that a disobedient animal was not the sort of thing I could countenance.

I called to him once more. He opened his eyes into slits and fixed me with a baleful glare from across the room. "Come here baby," I murmured. He continued to give me the evil eye. As I tried to out-stare him, a calming vision filled my mind in which I saw myself heaving him out the window. But I knew that I could never get away with that. My wife would know I was the murderer. And she was a vengeful little pig, more than capable of cutting my cock off as I slept or lacing my spaghetti and meatballs, which, oddly enough, she prepared perfectly, with rat poison.

Then my mind conjured the happy thought of tossing both of them through the window …. Snapping back to reality, I saw a jury and a small jail cell with a large Samoan calling me "dear" and I abandoned that idea. It then occurred to me to throw myself out the window. But who had the energy?

I got off the couch and ambled over to the cat. Now his eyes were fully open. He mewed as I gently scratched the top of his head and even purred, no doubt involuntarily. I could feel him tolerating me and plotting to destroy me. I was convinced that his claws were caked with poison that he would release with raking strokes into my flesh at the proper time, and that his feces in the cat box was filling the air with bacteria that were attacking me even as I petted him. And I knew he was planning to go on with my wife and another man long after my toxic body was lowered into a wormy grave.

I picked him up and carried him into the kitchen. He resisted but I held tight. I thought about putting him in the oven but decided the smell of burning cat flesh would be too noticeable and unpleasant. Then my gaze fell on the refrigerator and I carried him over to it.

"Motherfucker," I said, "my life is falling apart. Did you know that?" He was rigid as a board and his claws extended. "Yes, you little cocksucker, my life is over and you know why."

I opened the refrigerator and put him into the freezer compartment. He didn't resist. As I shut the door I thought of the white cleanliness of the Arctic tundra, a land of purification I had always intended to visit but never had. Well, at least he would.

I grabbed a box of Oreos and went back into the living room and stretched out on the couch. I sat staring out the window eating one cookie after another. Don't think me too far gone. I was aware of the depravity of my deed and was battered by wave after wave of guilt and misery. Yet what could I to do? It was me or him.

After fifteen minutes or so, I went into the kitchen and opened the freezer to see how he was doing. He sat on his haunches eyes glinting with hate, body shaking. Small icicles were forming on his whiskers.

"You haughty little fuck," I laughed. "Who's the master now?"

I shut the door and returned to the couch. I must have fallen asleep, for when I heard the creaking of the apartment door opening, darkness had coated the windows. I heard my wife calling to me, asking if I wanted a drink. A drink? Through cobwebs I realized she must be in the kitchen … the kitchen … something was wrong … wait … the kitchen … the refrigerator was in the kitchen … the refrigerator … the freezer ….

… and with horrible clarity I remembered what I had done. I scrambled off the couch and raced through the living room. I had almost reached the kitchen when a scream exploded from the depths of my wife's soul, a scream so deep and sorrowful it near split me in two.

I made a quick left-hand turn and raced into the bedroom. I dug some money out of a stash under the carpet. I was throwing some clothes into a flight bag when I felt, rather than heard, a presence behind me. I turned ….

…. and saw the frosty, ice-coated face of the cat hurtling toward me, fangs bared in a death attack. It was alive! I fell to my knees, ready for the fatal bite.

The cat flew by me, smacked into the wall, and broke into pieces, like porcelain. One of his little frozen paws landed on my knee. I looked up to see my wife looming over me. As my mouth worked to form an apology, I saw the steak knife in her right hand.

NICORETTE

There are times when I wish you and your new boyfriend would die. In his new Tesla, just fly off the road and roll over and explode. Instead, I am driving to his multi-million-dollar home outside of Scottsdale, Arizona, to spend Yom Kippur with both of you since, as your claim, I am your best friend and family. Yom Kippur is the only time of the year I commune with God, unless you count the prayers I utter every day at the racetrack. I am proud of my decision to join you and your new beau. I am now capable of moving beyond what I want and what I need. I can now be there for you more than I ever was in the relationship.

Just past Indio the AC in my twelve-year-old car stops working. Even with the windows down and dust swirling about me in a mini tornado, there is little respite from the one hundred plus heat. Who would live out here? Why didn't I fly? What's so special about spending countless hours in a machine in which one could cook a brisket?

When I reach a city named Blythe, I pull in at a rest stop. Two Wendy's cheeseburgers and a vanilla shake later I feel somewhat human. As I am about to get into my car, I think about the two of you. This new guy you're with is one of the good ones. Rich, smart, a social creature, and he can control, and enjoy his drinking. I've watched him. I watch people who drink. Even when your new beau has had a few and his speech is slurred, his personality does not change. Oh, maybe the jokes take longer to tell and the gestures more expansive. But he is never unkind. With me, three beers make me happy, and beyond that I am a man with a disease taking medication guaranteed to worsen the condition.

As I am reflecting on how lucky you are to have found someone like him, my reverie is interrupted by a female voice.

"Sorry to bother you. Can I bum a cigarette?"

It is a young girl, maybe 20's, in a t-shirt, jeans, black low-cut Cons, an oversized backpack in the shape of a panda at her feet. Her hair is black, short, skin unblemished, huge dark eyes, innocent, gamin-like. An old man's fantasy emerging from the sand.

"Don't smoke," I say. "Want a piece of Nicorette?"

"I'm not trying to stop."

"Neither am I," I say.

"Why do you chew it?"

I think about the first time I tried Nicorette. It was our second date. We were eating in an Italian restaurant in Brentwood. Waiters in white coats circled like birds of prey, Italian opera flowed through speakers, walls and lighting were frozen in crimson tones; a dinner blanched by the murmurings of profligate squalor. I a man incapable of learning from the past as you were planning the future. We laughed. Our eyes saw new things. You were holding this little piece of gum. Nicorette, you said. Can I try it? Sure, you said, and you gave me a piece. It burned my throat and made the top of my head sweat. Here it was, twelve years later, and I chewed countless pieces every day.

"It's kind of a habit," I said to the girl.

"I could use a ride," she said. "I'm heading to LA."

The desert was quiet, the whisper of arid nothingness offering chance.

"LA?" I said. "So am I. Just so you know, my car doesn't have air conditioning."

She shrugged and said, "Let me try a piece of that Nicorette."

BONDINI'S PLAN

Bondini was in the Pony Lounge nursing his eleventh scotch and soda. Even though he was drunk, Bondini could not escape the anxiety of knowing that soon he would be dead, for he was into some heavy characters for serious money which he could never repay, money that he had long since left at the crap tables in Atlantic City. For Bondini there was only the hope that his death would not be too lingering and cruel.

As he sipped, his eyes focused on a yammering face on the cheap TV. It was a doctor talking about a new surgical procedure which entailed implanting a small metal plate just inside the ear drum. The doctor was claiming to have helped many people, who for one reason or another, needed a metal plate inserted into their heads.

"By placing a thin piece of titanium just here," said the doctor, pointing with a baton to a Styrofoam skull, "one can insure the patient will resist almost any kind of blow to the skull. And that includes the impact of a small caliber bullet."

Bondini watched the doctor's mouth flap on and on but he had stopped listening after he heard that the plate could stop a bullet. That, thought Bondini, is just what I need.

The next day, Bondini got the doctor's name from the TV station and made an appointment. At the consultation, the doctor told him what he had told the TV audience, along with the cost of the operation: ten thousand dollars.

"Jeez, I ain't got that kinda dough," said Bondini.

"I take American Express, Visa, Mastercard, or Shell credit cards," said the doctor.

After financial arrangements were made Bondini said, "This operation is very important to me. I mean, are you sure I can take a bullet it the head and walk away like it was nothin'?"

"Not exactly," said the good doctor. "At the very least you will suffer a serious concussion and some loss of hearing. Of course, if the bullet enters at a certain angle more, ah, serious injury could result."

"But you could tell me where the bullet should go?" asked Bondini.

The doctor leaned back and regarded this curious patient.

"You know," said the doctor, "if I didn't know better I might think you were planning to get shot in the head."

That was Bondini's idea, of course, to get shot in the head. After that the plan was vague but it involved being taken somewhere and dumped and left for dead. Except instead of being dead he would get up and stroll off to a new life with nobody in pursuit.

Three days later during a six-hour operation, Bondini got a piece of titanium the size of a Reese's Peanut Butter Cup implanted just northeast of his left ear. After a suitable period of recovery, he contacted the mob.

"Little Sal," Bondini said, "I gotta see Lefty to work this thing out."

"Ain't no working out," said Little Sal.

Bondini described what he had in mind to Little Sal. All he wanted was the honor of killing himself. After all, hadn't he been a good soldier for a long time before his transgressions at the gaming tables? Little Sal was skeptical but when he called Bondini back it was with the news that Lefty had accepted the offer, as a gesture of appreciation for Bondini's contributions over the years.

"Just don't bring your own gun," said Little Sal. "Lefty'll get nervous if you're carrying."

"Sure thing," said Bondini. He forced back the urge to request a .22 caliber pistol for his execution. Instead he said a small prayer that the little plate in his head would deflect a larger caliber bullet.

At the appointed time, Bondini, wearing his finest silk suit, walked into Lefty's house. In short order Little Sal escorted him into the inner sanctum. Lefty rose from his desk and embraced Bondini.

"I am sorry, Dino," said Lefty, "that you must pay the ultimate price. However, what can I do? If I let you get away with ripping me off for two hundred large I lose all respect. But I appreciate your coming to atone for your sins and saving me the trouble of hunting you down like a dog."

With that Lefty pulled a gun from his waistband. Bondini nearly laughed when he saw it was a .22.

"May God have mercy on your soul," said Lefty.

He handed Bondini the gun. Without a word Bondini put it to the spot on his head, the exact center of the plate, the precise point where he had practiced putting the gun at least five thousand times in the last two months, and pulled the trigger.

The slug tore into his head. His brains went whizzing around the room like insects. He was killed instantly. Lefty and Little Sal gathered around Bondini's bloody, inert form.

"Fucking guy had balls," said Lefty. "Who woulda guessed it."

HAPPY BIRTHDAY

I was going on my thirteenth birthday—I remember because I was trying to memorize my Haftorah portion for my Bar Mitzvah, a task as impossible as dunking a basketball—when our next-door neighbor, Susan, would come over to play in our back yard with my younger brother and myself. Susan was cute as a button and a pretty good athlete.

Before long we took playtime up to my brother's room, where he would perform puppet shows for us. Susan and I would sprawl on his bed, hands touching, as he regaled us with idiotic plots featuring little ingenuity or coherence, traits that would later prove helpful in his Hollywood career penning scripts for *Knight Rider* and *Automan*.

I told my brother his shows would be more authentic conducted in the dark. He complied and I became emboldened. I touched Susan's miniscule breasts outside of her shirt, all the while attempting to tune out my brother's insipid yammering.

I convinced him to dispense with "intermission," during which he tried to sell us lemonade and cookies. I encouraged him to be more artistic and so he added action figures, stuffed animals, and fruits to the shows. This gave me more time to explore my budding passion.

I was soon groping Susan's small bare breasts. One day, I guided her hand to my rock hard shlong. The day I pulled my zipper down and she touched my bare whipper was my second tangible proof of God, the first being the ninth inning of a Junior Varsity baseball game when my team was down eleven runs and I prayed to God for victory and we scored twelve in the 9th to pull it out.

Speaking of pulling it out, as time went on Susan became bolder and it took her less than twenty quick pulls before I exploded in a frenzy of squeeze juice and joy. This went on for a couple of months like cock work.

One day, I was outside raking leaves when Susan and her father came strolling by our front lawn.

"Why hello, Paul," said her dad. Susan was staring at her shoes as if they had turned into lizards with rhinestone wings.

"Hi, Mr. Persky," I said.

"When you're finished raking, come over and have a piece of birthday cake. We're very proud of Susan. After all, she's seven years old today."

LIMOUSINE EXPERIENCE

Driving a limousine wasn't so bad. Not if you didn't mind interminable periods of sitting behind the wheel of an oversized Cadillac, one eye on a novel and the other out the window waiting for the customer. It was bit like trying to read in the dentist's office: one could never really concentrate. If the client got to the limo without my spotting them, upon hearing the click of the door opening I would leap out like a deranged jack-in-the-box, wildly trying to wrestle the handle out of their hand so I could do my job.

I worked for a fellow named Albert who was loud, rude, and obnoxious. Albert insisted I wear a beeper and be on call twenty-four hours a day. He wanted his chauffeurs ready to ride at any hour. Sometimes Albert would beep us for the hell of it, to make certain we were ready to be on call. I didn't mind. There was something about being paged in a public place that made me feel like a vital cog. I often let the thing beep on and on, making certain everyone knew it was me that was being paged. When all eyes were on me I would sigh and stalk off, making it clear that this electronic intrusion was insufferable to a man of my station.

One night, I was in bed with my girlfriend watching the *David Letterman Show*—a religious ritual for us—when the beeper went off. As I had no one to impress I cursed, lurched out of bed, and called Albert.

"It's Jim," I grunted when I got him on the line.

"Get a pen and paper," he said. "I have a pickup."

"Now?"

"No. Next fucking Purim. Of fucking course, it's now. Are you fucking ready?"

I muttered that I was.

"Go over to the garage. Get the red stretch. Should be clean but make fucking sure it's spotless. Make sure the bar is stocked. Then get to the Plaza and pick up a Mr. and Mrs. Putzsky. A two-hour job. They'll pay cash."

"Where are they going?"

"Up your fat ass," Albert fumed. "Just do the job. And be there in forty-five minutes." He slammed the phone down and the line went dead.

Forty-five minutes? He was some putz to think I could get to the Plaza and pick up the Putzkys by then. Since I was putzier, I threw on a shirt and tie and began squeezing into my one and only black chauffeur's suit. I'd been gaining a lot of weight and the pants were tight; they fit a bit like leotards. After hopping around for a while I managed to get the zipper closed. I slipped on my shoes and was halfway out the door when I realized I had forgotten to put on socks or underpants.

"There's nothing clean anyway," said my girlfriend as if reading my mind, never taking her eyes from the TV.

I sprinted the two blocks to the limo garage, all the while trying to put a knot in my tie. When I got there, I had managed to put a decent Windsor in the thing, perfectly formed, except it was the size of a softball.

By a miracle, the red stretch was clean. I leaned into the back and reached my full length to make certain the liquor decanters in the bar were filled. As I stretched to lift the gin bottle I heard a tremendous tearing sound.

My first thought was that I had ripped the upholstery and would have to leave town to escape Albert's fury. Then I put my hand around to my rear and was horrified to find I was petting bare skin. It seemed my pants had finally obeyed a basic law of physics and had split from crotch to waist, revealing, sans underwear, a goodly portion of my hairy, plump ass. As I didn't have another suit and had less than twenty minutes to get to The Plaza, I decided to chance it and hope for the best.

When I arrived at The Plaza I had to park down the block, as the front entrance was buzzing with taxis, horse-drawn carriages, and bozos from the Taxi and Limousine Commission. I got out and minced toward the hotel, hands clasped behind my back trying to pull the tattered edges of my pants together.

I shuffled across the lobby and announced to the concierge that the limo for the Putzkys had arrived. He got on the phone and shortly told me they'd be right down. While waiting, I glanced in the mirror and noticed the oversized Windsor knot had travelled around my shirt collar and was resting against my neck, making it appear as if I had a huge yellow goiter. I yanked the tie back into place and then, as urbanely as possible under the circumstances, shuffled back outside to wait for my customers. I double-parked the stretch in front. Within minutes an elegant couple emerged from the hotel.

"Good evening," called the man. "You are the driver Albert sent?"

I edged from the limo, approached, and began to bow—Albert insisted we bow—when a blast of artic air knifed through the hole in my pants, causing me to leap forward and land between them. They jumped back.

"Yes sir, I'm the driver. And it's my pleasure to be at your service this evening." Mr. Putzky was regarding me with a fearful expression, perhaps wondering if I would once again attempt to leap into his arms. They finally decided it was safe and moved toward the red stretch. I yanked the back door open and watched them get in, keeping my back away from them the entire time. Then I went around and slid behind the wheel, making a mental note to slide as little as possible for the remainder of the evening.

"Where to, sir?" I queried.

"We want to spend a couple of hours driving around Central Park. Nice and slow. Relaxing."

"And romancing," chimed in Mrs. Putzky.

"Yes sir, yes ma'm," I gushed. This was real luck. I'd only have to open the door for them one more time, when we returned to The Plaza at the end of the trip.

We entered Central Park. The Putzkys closed the small partition and I was left in peace to concentrate on keeping the car at a steady twenty miles an hour and not obliterating the horse drawn carriages that suddenly loomed in the darkness. We hadn't been on the road five minutes when the partition slid open.

"Driver, we can't get the gin decanter open."

"One moment, sir."

I guided the limo to the side of the road and put it in park. I swiveled and looked through the partition, which was only about a foot tall and a foot long, and down at the bar which was directly below. I reached through and tried manipulating the decanter but succeeded only in rearranging the ligaments in my armpit.

"Wouldn't you rather have whiskey this evening?" I said with a grin.

"Gin. We want gin," said Mrs. Putzky.

With I sigh I got out, went to the back door, opened it, and sized up the situation. It appeared the only way I'd have access to the bar was to climb into the back and crawl to it on my hands and knees. I'd just have to be certain to remain parallel to my customers in order to spare them a glimpse of the dark beyond. I entered, crawled into the car, got into position, and pulled the top of the gin decanter. It didn't budge. Moving forward I made another go at the top, but the damn jump seat prevented me from getting a good grip on the decanter. From the side angle, it appeared my efforts were doomed.

"You know," said Mrs. Putzky, "if we wanted to watch clowns we could have gone to the circus. And I daresay our friend Albert will learn of your incompetence."

Their *friend* Albert? The adrenaline started flowing and I soon was twisting, pulling, and yanking at the top with all my might. After what seemed like hours the thing popped free.

I examined it as a surgeon might a tumor he has removed from an important patient. With sweat pouring down my face I held the decanter top aloft and turned and faced the Putzkys.

"Yes," I said with a grin. "Bar's open."

They were staring at me wide-eyed and ashen faced. Absolute shock. In a flash, it dawned on me that as I was wrestling with the decanter my bare butt must have been wriggling in their faces. Mrs. Putzky moved her mouth but no words came out. Mr. Putzky had clearly entered a catatonic state, his eyes focused somewhere in the middle distance. I crawled backwards from the limo, shut the door, got in the front, and drove off.

They didn't say another word the rest of the trip. When I dropped them off they hurried away, eyes averted. I noticed the gin decanter was empty.

The next day Albert beeped me.

"How'd it go last night?" he asked.

"Pretty good," I said.

"Where'd they go?"

"Where you said they'd go."

"Where's that?" asked the mystified Albert.

"Up my fat ass."

I hung up.

SEVEN OF EVERYTHING

It's about seven. Seven shirts, pants, socks, underpants. Seven changes of clothes, one for each day of the week. The plan is Vegas to play the horses. Find out if I've got it.

This woman I have been dating for almost six years says I'm a race track junkie. She doesn't know the half of it. Of course I'm a junkie. Who would pass an adrenaline shot to the heart and a bliss ride down Doom Street fifteen or twenty times a day?

But I'm a great horseplayer. She doesn't know how good. For all the time I have been with her and her twelve year old daughter, I have been trying to be Mr. Good Daddy. Well, that's when I haven't been at the track. I think I've been with them for about ten minutes during daylight hours.

I'm around a lot at night. Sometimes we go out to dinner. I put away the food with both hands. They sort of move the food around with their forks, every once in a while, swallowing a strand of pasta. The bill comes for sixty bucks, what are you going to do? Force them to eat the shit?

I try to make conversation with the kid but she glares at me. Calls me fatty. That's okay, I was a great camp counselor and I know what's what. I'm a fun guy. Just 'cause real dad checked out when she was five doesn't mean she should take it out on me.

Seven of everything, in my Toyota Matrix. Just had an oil change. I trust my Toyota to take me anywhere, that is, anywhere there's not a breeze of more than thirty miles per hour. Over thirty and that aluminum piece of shit will lift off like a kite.

I decide not to say goodbye. What am I going to say? You were right, honey, I loved you and your daughter and your little dog but I'm a self-involved jerk? Even sober I'm a zero? Nah, it's better just to leave. One day, if I can figure out how to work the expensive Apple laptop she bought me, I'll send her an e-mail. For now, it's just seven changes and my Matrix. I leave my cell phone behind.

I head out the 10 Freeway, through the San Gabriel Valley, man it's desolate out here. Haze hangs over the rooftops. Past car lots, Home Depots, MacDonald's, Burger Kings, Del Tacos, everything is everything. Mom and Pop of former Mom and Pop stores must be holed up in trailers watching *Wheel of Fortune* and sipping arsenic cocktails waiting for the end. Then onto the 15 Freeway, asphalt loop de loop interchange, sign says "North to Barstow". How come it doesn't say north to Vegas? Who the fuck goes to Barstow? Maybe me in a year or two. Maybe I should stop and check it out. Nah, I'll get there when I get there.

As I'm zipping up the 15, I think of my girlfriend and the kid. They were a cute little duo. Fucked beyond recognition with neurosis and Brentwood greed and western intolerance to anything not au courant, but so cute and dreamy and innocent and desirable. I was their man, too, until I had a vision of myself in ten years with tubes coming out of my body and them visiting me in the hospital saying, "Well, you're not related to us, good luck." As cute as they were they'd always just tolerate me, that's all anyone does, especially as you get older.

And yet, as I pull off the freeway in some used-tire hellhole of a city, I find I miss them. Maybe it's something about myself I miss. I can't identify it. A sense of promise, no, of integrity....

Integrity? I wouldn't know integrity if I pissed on it.

There's a pay phone by Lance's Propane and Natural Gas. I pull the Matrix in, turn off the engine. Cars whiz by behind me. I pull a handful of quarters out of the glove compartment.

THE HERO

Robert Kintsner spent his days wandering about New York City looking for things to collect. Every few minutes or so he would yell FUCK YOU or FUCK YOUR MOTHER, depending upon his mood, to no one in particular. This startled people and occasionally angered them. But as soon as they saw Robert was a harmless old man, they turned away and left him muttering to himself as he peered inside a trash can or dumpster looking for some hidden treasure.

One summer afternoon, Robert found himself inside a bank stuffing deposit slips into the pockets of his woolen overcoat. He was about to start on withdrawal slips when two masked gunmen charged into the bank and announced a stickup.

One of them ran to the tellers' windows, leaped over the counter, and began scooping up cash from the drawers. The other trained his weapon on the dozen or so customers and ordered them onto the floor. Everybody complied, except Robert. He remained standing, stuffing little green slips into his pockets, watching the scene with as much interest as a grazing cow watches cars pass on a highway.

The gunman spotted Robert and motioned with his gun. Robert stood there, unaware of the tension that was thickening like cold grease.

"I'm not gonna tell you again, old man," barked the gunman. At that exact moment, for reasons which must remain conjecture, Robert felt the urge to vent himself.

"FUCK YOU," he yelled, at the same time spotting a pile of blue forms on the corner of the table. The gunman blinked in disbelief. He strode over to Robert and was about to ask him to repeat himself when Robert saved him the trouble.

"FUCK YOU AND YOUR MOTHER," Robert embellished and lunged for the forms, perhaps afraid that this angry person would reach them first.

It was this sudden move which saved his life. The bullet meant for his forehead nicked his ear. Robert screamed in pain. Forced into reality by having his ear lobe shot off, Robert grunted and leaped onto the gunman. The gunman tried to get off a second shot. But Robert was all over him, snarling and spitting like a rabid dog.

They fell to the floor, rolled around a bit, and ended up with

Robert sitting on the man's chest and yanking his nose with both hands. The other robber, sensing a bungled mission, sprinted from the bank, leaving his partner under the raving lunatic.

As soon as the second gunman fled the scene, the patrons scrambled off the floor and helped lift Robert off the dazed robber. They clamored about him offering medical attention and congratulations. Robert stood there, one hand on his injured ear, eyes glazed. He was returning to his pre-heroic state of virtual unconsciousness. The president of the bank, having just unlocked himself from his office, arrived on the scene and embraced Robert.

"My good man," he boomed, conducting a dress rehearsal for the six o'clock news, "your actions have been those of a hero, a man among men. This bank and all men of noble spirit owe you the deepest gratitude and undying thanks. Tell us, my good man, how you did it." As he spoke the president wondered from where the powerful smell of fecal matter was emanating.

Robert turned and looked at the president. Robert's eyes were pinwheels and his mind a tilt; spit flecked his lips and blood coursed from the bullet wound on his ear.

"FUCK YOU," said Robert. "FUCK YOU AND YOUR MOTHER."

WHITE HOUSE

I'd like to tell you about a remarkable occurrence of several years ago.

It began when I couldn't remember whether I had 38 or 48 dollars in my checking account. When I called to verify, a cheerful clerk informed me I had a balance of $4,967. She repeated this information eleven times for my disbelieving ears.

That afternoon I strolled in and withdrew $4,900. While the teller was counting out the money my heart was pounding so hard I was afraid blood was going to spurt from my nose. I managed to keep from clicking my heels until I was outside of the bank.

You see, this money represented freedom, a new life I envisioned in a comfortable Hollywood apartment, complete with a computer, and stories and articles pouring out of it, ensuring my financial and literary reputation.

A detour to Hollywood racetrack the following afternoon put a dent in my dreams. I bet $4,800 to place on a 2-5 shot, a horse everybody said couldn't lose. Nobody told the horse, and he finished fifth.

A week later the bank sent over a trio of tough-talking attorneys. They offered me a fine array of options, from prosecution for felony embezzlement to a repayment program of $500 a month. Utterly defeated, I chose the latter. In order to come up with the money, I was forced to supplement my work as a script reader with an evening job at a furniture store on Western Avenue, called, for no apparent reason, the White House.

I developed an immediate rapport with my co-workers, Rojelio and Chino. In spite of the tricks they shared, I managed to catch my scrotum in the hernia belt on a daily basis. At the end of each evening I ached all over, bruised and strained from repeated lifting of Ethan Allen furniture.

By the end of my second month at the White House, in a desperate attempt to alleviate the pain, I saw a chiropractor who wore a bright floral dress, resembled Carmen Miranda, and cracked my neck like castanets. The treatment had my head swiveling like one of those bobble-head dolls, but the pain continued unabated.

My sister-in-law convinced me toxins in my colon were causing my problems, so I went for a high colonic. During treatment, the doctor received an important phone call and forgot to remove the tube from my insides for a couple of hours. I was irrigated more thoroughly than a Malaysian rice paddy during monsoon season, and for weeks I dreamed of nothing but watermelons.

Rogelio recommended a Salvadoran herbologist who prescribed fifty or so natural remedies four times a day. Several of the pills were the size of gherkins. I stopped the program when I received the Heimlich maneuver at a Thai restaurant.

In a last ditch attempt at ameliorating the pain I went to a masseuse whose number I acquired from the *L.A. Weekly*. I experienced a cessation of pain during an unexpected hand job at the end of the massage. An hour later the aching resumed, along with a disturbing itching sensation along my inner thighs.

The bank had to be paid and I kept working at the White House. In the mornings I'd drag myself out of bed, wondering if most forty-year-old men crawled on their hands and knees to the bathroom. As the hot water of the shower played on my aching muscles, I felt the old "me" begin to ooze forth. After several cups of coffee, I arrived for work, ready to prove to Chino and Rogelio that an aging Jew was the equal of any piece of furniture.

One hot summer day, while attempting to prove I had the right stuff, I fell off a six-foot ladder with a lounge chair balanced precariously on my shoulders. All I could think about in the instant before I hit the floor was that if the chair was only beneath, instead of on top of me, I would have been fine. As it was, the chair landed on my back, driving me into the floor like a screw. It seemed as if I was under the thing for an eternity, my calls for help muffled by the excellent padding in the seat.

I'll never forget the look of horror on Chino's face when he lifted the chair and saw me beneath it. Normally endowed with a deep voice, Chino's screams rose several octaves until they sounded like a Minnie Riperton solo. As he and Rogelio lifted me to my feet I almost fainted, and thoughts of wheelchair basketball filled my mind.

While they were feeding me a bowl of menudo and a mug of Olde English Ale, an odd thing occurred. I felt a certain flexibility about my body. I wasn't quite ready for a decathlon but gosh, I felt damn good!

Over the next few weeks I got better and better, and the only time I hurt was the day I had to pay the bank their $500. My vision improved and I drove without glasses. Little hairs grew on top of my head where not a hair had grown for twenty years; even more remarkable, they were blond. After sex, instead of grumbling and going to sleep, my lover insisted on bringing me a bowl of frozen yogurt.

Rogelio noticed my new-found strength and began to insist on taking what I had begun calling the "leap of health". Against my better judgment, I let him talk me into it.

One night after work, Rogelio climbed the ladder and Chino and I loaded a Barca Lounger onto his shoulders. After making the sign of the cross, he flung himself from the ladder. We waited for his screams of agony to subside, but he experienced no real relief until the morphine kicked in at the hospital. The last I heard, his broken collarbones were mending well.

I didn't bother to pick up my last paycheck and I never notified the bank of my plans to leave town. I headed to Tampa, Florida, an action city I heard had Jai Alai and greyhound racing, in addition to a lovely thoroughbred racetrack.

A NIGHT ON THE TOWN

After Lugatz had the colostomy, he became withdrawn. Once a social animal with a propensity for human contact, he became a loner whose tastes ran to macabre novels and marinated meats. At some point, even in his despair at feeling less than human, he realized he needed to get back in the social mainstream. So, one night he rummaged about in his closet until he came upon his favorite gray pinstripe suit, a white shirt, and a red and silver paisley tie. He dressed and admired his image in the mirror. He couldn't even see the bulge of the colostomy bag on his side.

He walked out of his garden apartment, got into the car, and drove the short distance into town. He felt good when he was greeted at Maury's as if he had never been away. He felt even better after he consumed three gin gimlets. He was working on the fourth when he heard a voice behind him.

"Lugatz. Where have you been?"

He turned and saw it was Valerie, a girl he had shared some good times with in the not-so-distant past. She was short, blonde, and cute in a reptilian sort of way. More important, she didn't know about his operation. He decided she would be a good person upon whom to test the truth.

"I've been ill, Valerie," he said, "very ill. I went into the hospital for surgery and came out …"

"… to see me, didn't you?" said Valerie with a twinkle in her beady little eyes.

Lugatz paused. Fuck the truth.

"Yes," he said. "I came out to see you, drink with you, and be carnal as hell with you. Still drink martinis?"

"Yes," giggled Valerie.

For a while, they sat and drank and enjoyed each other's company.

"Here's to life and anyone who can enjoy it," declared Lugatz, clinking the glass that contained his tenth gimlet against hers with such force that it sent most of her drink into her lap.

"To life," said Valerie lifting her half-filled glass to her lips.

They decided to repair to his place to continue where they had left off before he went into the hospital. They managed to get from the bar to the car and to his house without injuring themselves or anyone else, which was a miracle considering their condition, and after becoming lost in the shrubbery of his front yard, made their way to his bedroom. When they got there, she informed him she had to go to the little girl's room.

"Just wanna douche," she said with a moist, lumpy smile.

Lugatz smiled back, feeling grander than he felt a man had a right to feel. While Valerie was in the bathroom he undressed, and when she came out he was lying on the bed stroking his polyurethane colostomy bag, wondering if he should empty it before they had sex.

"What the hell is that?" Valerie shrilled.

"It's me," said Lugatz. "It's what they did to me in the hospital. But this," he added, holding his engorged penis, "this is still A-okay."

"What is that bag?" said Valerie.

"I no longer use my rectum," said Lugatz, "so my shit passes into this bag which I empty when it's full. It's no big deal."

Valerie had eaten beef stroganoff and apple pie for dinner. It and most of the martinis she had been drinking during the evening burst from her mouth in a choppy spray.

"Valerie," said Lugatz in a small, forlorn voice.

"Ahhhhh," said Valerie, unleashing a second helping of the nefarious stroganoff.

She tottered back and collapsed in a heap in a corner of the room. Lugatz stared at her and rubbed his penis with great vigor but couldn't ejaculate. He gave up and went into the bathroom to empty his colostomy bag.

When he came out he crawled under the sheets and thought about his childhood dreams of becoming a great writer and popular person.

Try as he might, he could not get to sleep.

MY THERAPY

My court ordered therapy wasn't going well. Dr. Fromer, my beautiful therapist, sat behind her desk saying nothing except "Do you see?" every once in a while. I was never sure if she was talking to me or to the monkey in the corner, a feral creature restrained by a three-foot chain manacled to its wrist.

I'd been thinking about killing Dr. Fromer. Maybe she could read my mind because at a recent session there was a large syringe and a straight razor on her desk.

"You know, Doc, when the shit comes down those trinkets on your desk ain't gonna help you."

Dr. Fromer glanced at the monkey. "Do you see?"

That got me. "You can talk to the fucking monkey but not to me? I'm the one that's paying you, you cocksucker, not that goddamn simian." At these words the little beast flew into the air trying to savage me, and I was very grateful for hard steel and willing fixtures.

One night I attended a dinner party hosted by Dr. Fromer. There were ten of us at the dining room table, excluding the monkey who was chained to a highchair on her right. I was enjoying a delicious linguine and meatballs until a rage filled me when I shook the parmesan container and it was empty. I was too ashamed to ask for more. Fucking monkey.

A gorgeous woman sat to my left. She had to be thirty years my junior, although these days everybody seems to be thirty years my junior. As I was helping myself to flan, I felt the woman's finger trace a line up my leg, under my shorts, and stroke my nut sack. It was bliss. She smiled and I observed her back teeth were gray and decaying. My desire evaporated. Dr. Fromer glanced at the monkey and said, "Do you see?"

But it was I who saw. I saw the imprint of perfection that could never be, attached like that monkey's chain around my every expectation and chance of happiness.

After the monkey died, I took the position. Every Thursday, Dr. Fromer gives me a sweet potato and a hand job. Day after day I watch the folly of human intention, the whining and lack of acceptance that characterize the human condition.

Dr. Fromer's patients are lucky my chains are strong.

VIOLETS

One Saturday night I was checking in at the La Jolla Hyatt. The lobby was teeming with pretty, young people. The women were mostly blond with toned legs set off by skin tight dresses cut just beneath the mounds of pubis. The dudes were dressed in baggy black clothes, wore vacant expressions, and appeared to have futures in waste management. The desk clerk told me it was a homecoming dance, whatever that was.

After I dumped my bag in my sumptuous room, which featured a huge TV, I wandered down to the lobby, took a seat in the corner, and watched the flesh parade. To my right was a garden featuring violets in little boxes. Violets, like the ones Aunt Francis had, the aunt I would visit when I was young, and late at night the bitch would come into my room and hold me and unleash the pecking pigeons from between her legs, and as they clawed and tore at me the only thing that saved me was the sight of those violets on the bureau.

My reverie was interrupted by a beautiful young creature.

"Excuse me," she said. "I don't mean to bother you."

"You couldn't bother me if you took a shit in my ravioli," I murmured.

"What? What did you say?"

"Why don't you take a load off?" I said. "Those heels look uncomfortable." I patted the seat next to me. She sat down.

"I have a bet with my boyfriend," she said. "I said you're Larry David. From, you know, that TV show."

"Close," I said. "I'm his older brother David. David David. I figure out the episodes and select the pastries for the buffet. Why don't you come by the set for a Danish?"

"My God," she gushed.

I asked if she had seen the episode about the Moyle who works for tips. She missed that one. Her name was Sue from Chula Vista. I told her what room I was in, in case the dance got boring. I figured I had a better chance of urinating gold ingots than of Sue showing up.

At 11:33 on the Sanyo clock by my bed there came a tapping at my door. It was Sue, shoes in one hand and a bottle of champagne in the other.

"Come on in," I said. "I was just coming up with story ideas."

Sue bounced in and plopped down on the bed. A half hour later we had polished off the booze and were old friends. When I went to kiss her, she pulled back.

"Whoa, Dave. I only kiss my boyfriend. But I can jerk you off."

I ran to the bathroom and got the courtesy bottle of lotion. With a frown on her face and left hand moving like a metronome, Sue got me off in no time.

I must have passed out for when I opened my eyes, she was gone. I looked at the little bottle of lotion by my thigh. I picked it up and squirted some into my hand. For some reason, I thought of violets.

THE GOD PLAN

"There was this guy in prison," said Emulus. "Atascadero, solitary confinement for four years."

"Sounds like my college career," I said.

"5 by 8-foot cell. Three squares a day and little else. Except for an *Almanac*. When they let him out, I think his name was Finnegan, he was a fact machine. If Finnegan could have got on *Jeopardy* he would've broke the bank."

"What happened to him?"

"He had this scam where he'd act drunk and stupid and bet the locals on trivia. Some yokel in a downtown bar caught onto the scam and hit him with a plank. You hungry?"

I was hungry, all right, but it wasn't for food. Finnegan had the hustle but he couldn't sell it, and selling a scam was the key. We went to Norm's on La Cienega. While I ate kept thinking about Finnegan.

"I wonder why he couldn't sell that hustle."

"Maybe he needed a magic wand," said Emulus.

I ignored the sarcasm. The words "magic wand" resonated but I wasn't sure why.

After we ate, we went to a theater on Hollywood Boulevard that played reruns for 7 bucks. I was enjoying a movie called *Meet the Parents* when this actor Owen Wilson appeared. He played a smart, good looking religious type. Yet, he had no charisma, no magic. No charisma. No magic. Bingo.

Over coffee at a Starbucks on Sunset, I revealed the way out of poverty. "It's simple, Emulus," I said. "All we have to do is find The Son of God and we'll be on easy street."

"God, as in God?"

"I don't mean God like Buddha or what's in this latte. I mean a walking, talking emissary of true faith. Listen, what with Trump getting elected, these are scary times. What do people always want?"

"I don't know," he said. "Raisinets?"

"*Hope*," I said. "People want hope. And what gives people more hope than anything? Faith. All we need is somebody with Owen Wilson's looks, Finnegan's smarts, charisma, and a magic wand and we'll have our very own Son of God. We won't be able to count the money fast enough."

"A magic wand," asked Emulus. "That was my idea."

Three weeks later, I found our guy at The Magic Castle in the form of a handsome young magician named Gary Memblis. The guy turned a duck into a monkey and I was sitting five feet away. How he knew I wasn't wearing underpants I'll never know. He had the smooth patter, too. In between keeping us laughing, he revealed he had several degrees from Harvard but magic was his passion. Gary was handsome. Had charisma. Had the smarts. And a magic wand. It was just a matter of working out the hustle.

We took him out to eat. He was down on his luck. The magic wasn't paying the bills and his girlfriend left him. After four Heinekens, I popped the question.

"Gary, how'd you like to be The Son of God?"

"Sure," he said. "What does it pay?"

I laughed. He laughed. His smile lit up Barney's Beanery. A fat biker who last smiled when he beat a rival gang member with a chain, smiled. A loser with three teeth paused before shooting the eight ball and grinned. Our boy had the charisma, alright.

After three months of rehearsal, we started renting clubs in small towns outside LA. Arandi—that was the stage name we gave Gary—came out in a flowing green robe and spun a riveting tale involving alternate solar systems, An Army of Fervent Angels, and an upbringing on a space station. As Gary spoke he flashed that hypnotic smile. Every once in a while, he'd wave his arms and a bird would fly out from under his armpit or smoke would rise from an audience member's head or Gary would levitate a few feet into the air. The crowed was mesmerized. Gary's last words before leaving the stage to the electronic sounds of Tangerine Dream and purple strobe lights were "Am I The Son of God? You decide."

Within a month, we were filling 70 seat clubs at $15 a head. An article in the *LA Weekly* entitled "Son of God Performs in Hesperia" gave us a boost.

Except it got weird, and fast. Within a month, Emulus and I almost died. There was a flume boat ride at Knott's Berry Farm that flew off the tracks and pinned us under the hull for ten minutes. And a nurse saved Emulus with the Heimlich after a chicken nugget got stuck in his throat at a KFC on Vermont.

"Maybe God's not happy with our scam," Emulus said while we

were waiting for Gary at a club in Barstow.

"Don't be a superstitious idiot," I said. "We're on Easy Street." As I spoke, a huge light fixture fell from the ceiling and crashed to the floor between us. Emulus needed 30 stitches in his forehead and I received an unwanted vasectomy.

I kind of lost touch with Gary and Emulus. A couple of years later, I was convicted of a crime I did not commit—I swear the girl said she was 18, although maybe the Barbie doll collection was a tip off — but solitary confinement isn't so bad.

I've got an in with a guard and any day now I'm supposed to get an *Almanac*.

ACCEPTANCE

She thought she was such an intellectual. Yeah, she thought, she thought, she thought about everything. I gave her flowers, a nice bouquet, cost me eight bucks in one of those subway flower shops. You can get a helluva bouquet for eight bucks at one of those places. I mean, for a fin you can get a bunch of good looking flowers you wouldn't be ashamed to bring to a sick relative in the hospital. Imagine what that eight-dollar number looked like.

So, I gave them to her. She looked at them as if she was biologist examining a specimen on a slide.

"What are these for?" she asked.

"Whaddaya mean, what are they for?" I replied, very pleasant like, keeping calm. "They're a token of my appreciation."

"And what is it you appreciate, William?"

Well, that stopped me cold. I couldn't say "your sweet pussy," could I?

"I don't know, honey," I responded. "It's everything about you. Your hair, your personality, the way you do things, the way you keep yourself. I like you for you and I gave you the flowers just for that."

Not bad, huh? But even as I said this, I could see the wheels turning. She ran her fingers across her forehead and back through her long dark hair. I loved when she did that.

"I cannot accept the flowers, William," she said, "because you're an insincere man. You come into my home and profess a regard for me that doesn't exist."

"But honey—"

"Your inability to lie is exceeded only by your lack of respect," she concluded.

I felt like saying, okay, fuck you, give me the flowers back. But something told me to keep quiet. After a minute or two she came close and put her arms around me. The bouquet fell from her hands.

"God help me, I need you," she whispered, lips touching my ear. "But please, darling, no more flowers, no more lies."

Just her closeness got me hard. In no time at all, we had our clothes off and were clawing at each other like animals. When I felt her come, when her screams and moans of pleasure shook the walls, I let myself come into her.

Five minutes later she turned back into fucking Plato.

"Oh yes, William, you're a great lover, a great man," she said, staring straight up at the ceiling. "A prideful little man who can make me happy in bed …. Remember something, my darling: it is your absurd feeling of sexual superiority that will destroy you. In order to be happy, you must be the equal of your partner. No more, no less."

I heard her, but from a very great distance. The sex had been too good. She could say anything she wanted. In fact, she could set it to music and sing it if that pleased her. Her pussy was all that mattered. And it was my cock she wanted in it.

We had a date later in the week. She came to the door wearing a very short skirt and a fishnet blouse with no bra.

"I thought we'd stay in tonight," she said, taking my hand and leading me into the living room.

In a vase, near the window, I saw the bouquet of flowers that I had brought to her last time. They looked great, worth at least fourteen, fifteen bucks.

THE SISTERS

He liked to sit on her balcony, drink beer, and stare into the sky. When the wind was strong the puffy clouds whipped by like feelings. He spent hours like this until she called him for dinner.

Once inside, the claustrophobia hit. Her large one-bedroom overlooking La Brea felt like a matchbox. As if through mud, he trudged to the dining table. Her little girl Emily sat at his right. She served the pasta and sat on his left. Sometimes he felt the need to say a prayer but nothing came into his head.

Usually they ate in silence. Sometimes, he made an effort.

"What did you do in school?" He was pretty sure she was in the fourth grade.

"Studied," the little girl said. She sucked a strand of pasta through the gap between her front teeth. The slurping sound enraged him. He wanted to bang her little face in. He was tired of being treated like a second-class citizen in his own home.

"What did you study?" he asked, chewing a perfectly cooked meatball.

"Oh, math and English. Spanish. Uno, dos, tres."

"That's good," he said. Fucking wetbacks. Soon English would be a second language.

"How about you?" he asked his girlfriend. "What'd you do today?"

She kept on eating, concentrating on her pasta as if she was an air traffic controller and the food a radar screen.

"I'm talking to you," he said, louder. She looked up.

"I worked," she said. "I always work."

"Are you back-talking me?"

"No. You asked what I did. I'm telling you."

"Cause there's no room for a rebellion here, sweetheart. Nobody's rising up in apartment 2002 at 1045 North La Brea."

"What are you talking about?"

He grabbed her chair and tilted it backward. She reached for the edge of the tablecloth. She managed to keep from toppling over but succeeded in dragging the bowl of linguine and meatballs onto the floor.

"Look at the mess," he said.

"I'll clean it," she said and went into the kitchen. The little girl put her fork down.

"Why do you hurt my mommy?"

"I don't hurt anybody. She brings it on herself."

"No. You yell at her and hurt her all the time."

"You want to know the truth? I don't know. Your mother is a wonderful woman and you're a wonderful girl. I need everybody to be good, that's all. If everybody would be respectful and listen then we'd have a happy household. C'mon, how about ice cream for dessert. I saw your mother bought chocolate malt. With fudge sauce, okay cutie pie?"

"Because my sisters don't like you hurting my mommy," the little girl said. "They told me so."

"You don't have sisters," he said. "Except in your head."

"Oh no," she said. "Amy and Cynthia are very real. They're very sad about how you treat my mother."

"That's enough. You'll go to your room. Leave the table. No ice cream."

The little girl got up and walked toward her room. She paused and turned at the doorway.

"One day you'll be sorry." She ran out.

He went into the kitchen, took off his belt, and tried to beat his girlfriend in the ass. He held her by one arm and struggled to keep her pinned, but she was strong and pounded him back. "Spill the damn food," he yelled as he tried to land a few good ones.

Then he went out onto the balcony and watched the sky. Clouds in the shapes of animals drifted across a fairy meadow. Look, there was a sheep, a zebra, a furry bear, several rabbits, cavorting, dancing, spirit dreams in a desert of woes. When he came in it was dark. He heard the scratching of the cello. The kid seemed to like playing that godforsaken thing.

He went into the bedroom to discover his girlfriend lying on the bed watching a TV show. She was dressed in a frilly black bra and thong. He stripped to his underpants, came and stood beside her. She turned, pulled his underpants down and gave him a blow job. He came within a minute or two, grabbing the back of her head as he pulsed in her mouth. God, he thought, she gives great head. He looked at the pile of money on the dresser. He counted it as the ten o'clock news was starting.

"Four-forty?" he asked.

"Yeah," she answered. "Two new girls started today. They took a few calls I might have had."

"Hey, you gotta work that moneymaker while you got it," he said, slapping her ass. She grinned and snuggled into his arms and kissed his neck.

"Don't kiss me," he said. "Not after you suck me off."

"Oh, excuse me," she said. "How do you think I feel?"

"Blessed and lucky," he said, "lucky and blessed."

Her attention was diverted to a headline. "Look at that," she said. "Another train crash."

"Safer to fly even with the Muslims."

"Can't even take a goddamn train."

They watched the litany of tragedies, holding hands. He could feel her fingers lightly moving against his fingertips, but he was too tired. He turned away but couldn't sleep.

"She keeps talking about sisters," he said.

"Emily?"

"Yeah. Emily. All the time with the sisters. What sisters?"

"It's a little girl's fantasy," she said. "That's all."

"I know that. But why?"

"I don't know, maybe she wishes she had sisters. Would you like to give her a sister?"

"I'd rather be dead," he said.

"That's lovely."

"You know what I mean. I'm not into that shit."

"Maybe someday when I stop working you'll feel different."

"Sisters, sisters, sisters."

"Well … she was going to have sisters." He heard something shift in his soul and move between the crosshairs of his attention.

"Tell me about it."

"I was pregnant with her. I went for the test to see if it was a boy or girl. They tell me it's all girls. All girls? Three of them. Triplets. I was going to have goddamn triplets!" The moment was an hourglass, tipped upside down, and sand was drifting slowly toward his open, parched, mouth.

"I was freaked, I was out of my mind. Triplets, for Goddsakes. You know, I wasn't into the life yet and Dennis was barely putting food on the table with his stupidass job at the aerospace plant. The poor schnook begged me to have all three, but it was a no brainer. I aborted the other two and kept Em. She's a keeper, don't you think?"

A God inside him smiled and asked for permission to embrace a distant memory. There were tears in his eyes.

"Did you have names for them?" he asked.

"It never got to that. I just wanted them out of me. Are you okay? Why, you're crying."

She crawled over his shoulder and watched him. She thought they were tears of sympathy and was filled with warm feelings. She sucked his breasts and played with his ass the way he liked, but when she heard the snoring she went to sleep as well.

Sometime later he was on the balcony waiting for her, thinking of the ways she had abused him. Twice she had failed to cook the meatballs properly. She hadn't offered a blowjob in almost a week. There was never toilet paper on the spindle and the dishwasher wasn't emptied.

And this was after he had felt closer to her. That was the problem. You get close to somebody and they take advantage. It was always the way. He'd give her a piece of his mind when she came home.

He watched animal clouds dance across the sky. An ominous bank of gray rainclouds pin-wheeled behind a flock of low-hanging cloud-ducks. He strained forward, interested in a lustrous vision.

Beneath the ducks, floating, emerged two little beautiful angel girls, willowy, beckoning with honeyed arms, long blond hair waving in the wind. They called to him, invited him, offered love and forgiveness. Their every gesture was a world of innocent hope and their beauty was cleansing and timeless, and his longing was overwhelming, and he climbed onto the balcony ledge and reached for them and went plummeting twenty floors to the pavement below.

THE DOCTOR'S PROBLEM

The big, white BMW carrying Dr. Paul Goldberg, Chief of Internal Medicine at Kings County Hospital, glided down Flatbush Avenue, in Brooklyn, New York. The good doctor was at peace, surrounded as he was by the smell of top grade leather and the strains of a Mozart concerto coming through the speakers. On this spring morning, he was feeling wonderful, as his girlfriend Midge had given him an excellent blow job just before he left her Upper East Side apartment.

Dr. Goldberg gazed out the window at the filthy streets, which even at this early morning hour seemed to be filled with clusters of roving black youths who glared at him with unconcealed hatred. I guess they don't know I'm the one who sews them up after they've been shot or stabbed, he thought. I'm the one who saves their lives. And for what? So, they can hate me?

While stopped for a red light at the corner of Myrtle and Flatbush, re-living the finer moments of the blowjob for perhaps the twenty-fifth time, a black face loomed at his window. Frozen with fear, the doctor watched as the man lifted something metallic and aimed it at him—but then swung it away and began scrubbing the windshield with a dripping squeegee. He felt his chest knot up and then jammed his foot on the accelerator and jetted through the intersection. He didn't glance back to see what happened to the man.

An hour later, in his office, the incident was forgotten. Rounds would begin and he had countless messages. In a neat pile were a stack of X-rays and tests that had come back from the lab. He was behind schedule and he knew there was only one way to deal with the situation.

He picked up his custom-made putter and strolled over to the little patch of Astroturf beside his desk and began banging balls into the practice hole he had set up for himself. Boink. Boink. Boink. Ball after ball rolled into the cup and was spun back by the electric return. He couldn't wait to get out on the course that weekend. He had a powerful feeling he'd get his score down under a hundred. The voice of his receptionist crackled through the intercom.

"Doctor, it's Mrs. Kinnerly again."

"She doesn't have an appointment, does she?" said Dr. Goldberg.

"No sir, but she says it's urgent."

He sighed. Mrs. Kinnerly was the mother of seven-year-old Clarence Kinnerly. A month ago, Clarence was shot in the head during a shootout between rival gang members in front of his Coney Island tenement. Now he was in a coma, the bullet having torn up his brain.

Goldberg knew the boy would never regain consciousness. But the woman, like all mothers, had heard of some treatment or drug that she wanted to try. They all wanted a fucking miracle. He had wanted miracles too as a young, idealistic doctor.

"Tell her to make an appointment. Tell her to—"

The door flew open. A slight black woman wearing an apologetic expression on her weathered face stood in the doorway.

"I'm sorry to barge in on you, doctor. I know you're busy …" Her gaze travelled to the golf club in his hand. For a moment neither spoke. "I need to speak with you about my boy."

"Clarence," he said.

"Yes. Could you spare a minute? Please?" He motioned her to a chair and shuffled some papers as she arranged herself.

"Yes, Mrs. Kinnerly?" he said. "What can I do for you?"

"I just came from my son's room," she said. "My Clarence is gone forever, isn't he?"

"Yes," he said. "I'm afraid I've never seen anyone come back from that kind of injury." She looked down, gnarled fingers clutching a vinyl purse.

"I appreciate your honesty, doctor." He nodded. At the moment, he was contemplating where he would take Midge for dinner. Would it be paella at Sevilla or a steak at Peter Luger's?

"I don't want Clarence to live like this," said Mrs. Kinnerly. "It hurts me too much. That's why I've come here to ask you to put him out of his misery."

"What's that?" Goldberg wasn't certain he'd heard her right.

"I want you to make my boy die," she said.

He sat up straight. "Mrs. Kinnerly, I understand what you're going through. But I'm a doctor. I have a commitment to keep my patients alive."

"But why?" said Mrs. Kinnerly. "You don't think he's going to get better."

"He probably won't. But I took an oath. And that's that."

She stood up. "I appreciate your time. I'll pray about this."

She turned and left the office. He leaned back in his chair and tried to focus on pleasant thoughts of sex, golf, and lunch. But the image of a little black boy hooked up to a respirator crowded into his head and pushed out everything else.

On rounds, Goldberg found he couldn't wait to get to Clarence Kinnerly's room. Once there, he studied the chart. No advanced directive and the boy was beyond help. On the way out a nurse said, "We're doing everything we can, doctor."

"Of course," he replied.

At about seven p.m., he took the elevator down to the basement and walked through the deserted parking garage. He was just opening the door to his BMW when three young black men materialized and surrounded him. One was tall, one was fat, and one was wearing a Yankees baseball cap. Their faces were smooth and untroubled. Dr. Goldberg was surprised he found them handsome.

"Give it up, motherfucker," the tall one said. He aimed his arm at the doctor, a paper bag concealing something in his hand.

"Of course," said the doctor. He pulled out his wallet and handed it over. He pried off a ring, then his watch.

"Motherfucking Rolex," said the fat boy, holding it up to the light.

"Motherfucking bagel eating motherfucker," said the tall one. He took a quick step forward and punched Dr. Goldberg in the mouth. The boys ran off. Dazed, the doctor pressed his hand to the wound, noting the blood streaming through his fingers. He sat down on the fender of the Beamer and felt anger course through him like a river.

The next day he came into the office with a butterfly bandage covering seven stitches on his upper lip. He hadn't slept and it wasn't because Midge had worked him over. He had been thinking about the Kinnerly boy. He had Sadie call the boy's mother and ask her to come in.

An hour later there was a knock at his door and Mrs. Kinnerly entered. He waited until she was seated.

"I've been reconsidering," he said. She watched him carefully.

"I'm going to honor your request," he said. The woman clasped her hands.

"Praise Jesus, doctor .... Praise Jesus."

'Then it's decided," he said.

She nodded and in a thin voice asked, "How will you do it? Do we have to go to court?"

"Oh no," said Dr. Goldberg. "I'll take care of it."

After work, the doctor locked himself in his office, read the *Wall Street Journal* and sipped from a glass of Dom Perignon. At exactly 11:45 p.m., he made his way to Clarence Kinnerly's room. Once there he switched off the respirator. The boy began to gasp. He clasped his hand over the boy's mouth. The boy began wheezing and his eyes bulged. For a moment, it appeared they would pop out of his head. Then, with a shudder, the boy fell still.

Dr. Goldberg felt disquieted, almost disappointed. Dispatching the boy hadn't been exciting at all. He had turned to go when he heard breathing coming from the bed. He turned and saw the boy's chest rising and falling. For a moment, Dr. Goldberg thought he was seeing things. He took the boy's pulse: a strong eighty beats a minute. He opened an eyelid and shined in a beam from a penlight. The dilation was profound, the coma persisted. And yet the child had come back from the dead.

Dr. Goldberg opened the door a crack and peered up and down the hall. Clear. He re-connected the respirator, crept out of the room, and left the hospital.

The next day, he told Mrs. Kinnerly that a family crisis had prevented him from doing the deed and told her he'd take care of it that night. As the day went on he found he was looking forward to dispatching the little rascal. He construed the boy's failure to die as an act of defiance. But tonight would be different. A few hundred cc's of a potent muscle relaxer would send the lad on his way. It was the kind of "accident" that happened in hospitals all the time.

At about two in the morning, Dr. Goldberg snuck out of a laundry closet and into the boy's room. He pulled a syringe from his lab coat and plunged it into the child's heart. The boy jiggled on the bed like a crazed marionette for a couple of seconds and went still. Now you're gone, Clarence, by my hand, the hand of your doctor. The hand that gave you life, has taken it from you.

As Dr. Goldberg turned to leave, the child began breathing again—long, deep breaths, normal and full. The doctor staggered back, clutching his chest. He pulled the empty syringe from his pocket, stared at it. Phenobarbital, enough to kill a horse. Was this some kind of sick joke? Was he losing his fucking mind?

He put his hands around the child's throat and squeezed until he felt the larynx bend like a licorice stick. When he let go, the child's tongue lolled out, bloated and purple as a fat Italian sausage. Dr. Goldberg stared at the boy, waiting to see what would happen.

He didn't have to wait long. With a loud blurp, moisture bubbles leaked from the sides of Clarence's mouth and he began to breathe again. The doctor ripped the respirator from the bed and lifted the child by the shoulders.

"Listen to me, young man," he snarled. "I'm in charge here. I'm the fucking doctor." He smacked the boy twice in the face as if to knock some sense into him.

Out in the hall the on-duty nurse heard a commotion coming from room 832. When she entered, she saw a man in a medical gown resembling the Chief of Internal Medicine running toward the window like a deranged halfback with a little black boy tucked in the crook of his arm like a football. Before she could react the doctor and the boy went crashing through the plate glass window.

The first person to reach them was Dr. Steven Farbelstein, a first-year resident. One look told him the adult was dead, his head crushed. But the little boy was alive. The man must have cushioned the blow. A gathering crowd of locals watched as the resident lifted the little boy and carried him toward the hospital. Their stares of hatred bored holes in his back.

REVERENCE

I couldn't concentrate on television. Maybe it was because I was going to meet my girlfriend's parents for the first time. It wasn't that I was nervous or apprehensive. In fact, I was looking forward to her mom's home cooked vittles. I just couldn't concentrate. My girlfriend, on the other hand, was working herself into a panic, albeit a quiet one. She said not a word as she tried on several blouses, arranged and rearranged her hair, and rummaged through countless shoeboxes. As she passed between me and the TV for the tenth time in order to examine herself in the mirror, I became enraged at her lack of consideration. I almost said something but, I thought, hey, she's nervous that we're going to see her folks. I'll take the high road. Although the smell of her perfume, which wafted across the room like a fart each time she whipped past, nauseated me.

When she was finally ready, she asked how she looked and I said beautiful. She didn't look bad, the black suit was well cut and made her ass appear smaller. But her feet looked silly in those flats she favored—shiny flats that made her feet look huge.

On the car ride over I was concerned that we hadn't much to say. I was hoping to be brimming with conversation in preparation for her folks. She put on a Motown compilation CD. I'd heard each of the songs eight billion times. But she went on singing along in a reedy voice, "My girl, my girl, talkin' 'bout my girl …."

We stopped at a 7-11 and I bought a Diet-Coke. I sipped like it was champagne. The 101 wasn't too crowded and we made it out to Westlake in less than an hour. Down a boulevard, several side streets, and to a small, middle class country-style home.

"Remember, my mother's a little hard of hearing," she reminded me for maybe the sixth time.

"I know," I said. "I'll be sure to cup my hands."

"You don't have to mock me."

"I was kidding around. Sorry."

When we were halfway up the sidewalk she stopped. "Didn't you forget something?"

"I did?"

"The flowers."

"Oh yeah." I went back, opened the trunk and saw that during the trip a milk crate full of papers had fallen onto the bouquet, crushing it.

"Jesus Christ," she said when I returned. "What happened to the flowers?"

"It's the thought that counts," I said.

"It was *my* thought and *my* flowers."

They greeted us at the door, her mom and dad, looking old, trim, jocular, and well dressed. They took our coats and ushered us into the den. They fixed me up with a V-8 and their daughter with a big glass of Merlot. They had martinis. We clinked glasses and I winced when my girlfriend said, "L'Chaim."

"L'Chaim," we chimed in.

After we drank, her dad said, "Ruth told us you do corporate picnics."

"Yes, sir, I have my own company and I'm proud to say we're in our tenth year."

"That's a great accomplishment," he said.

"Grown every year, too," I said.

"Still better."

"Have you ever been to one of Paul's picnics, Ruthie?" her mom asked.

"Yes, I went to one in July," said Ruth. "It was, ah, interesting."

"Ruth saw one of our less professional efforts," I said. "Someone forgot to put dry ice in the ice cream cooler and so … well…"

"And the clown was in the shade sleeping," said Ruth with a smile.

"The clown was adjusting to a new estrogen regimen," I said. "But she's fine now. All in all, people had a good time."

"They always do," Ruth said. "Paul's company spares no expense to ensure the happiness of the clients."

"It's true," I said. "Most of my clients are thrilled. This is a beautiful house, Mrs. Grubbs." Her mother's eyes were twinkling more brightly with each sip of booze.

"Oh, it's just our little place but we're comfortable. I understand you two have talked about getting your own place."

"I enjoy living in my office," I said. "That way, if I want to work at three, four in the morning I can."

"It's interesting the way you phrased that," her mother said. "Living in your office. Most people talk about living at home and working in an office."

"No, my apartment is an office, first and foremost," I said. "I am committed to my business. After all, if I don't look after it, who will?"

I smiled at her mother. "You have a beautiful crystal collection."

"Thank you," she cooed. "Primarily Lalique, although Baccarat is represented. Baccarat is doing wonderful things with small animals these days."

"Are you happy doing what you are doing?" asked her father.

"I enjoy my work but I don't believe in happiness," I said. "Too many people waste time looking for happiness. I think every moment I'm on this planet is blessed." I looked over at Ruth, caught the bad left profile. I eased my hand out of hers.

"That's a marvelous philosophy," her mother said. "Glass half-full, not half-empty."

"Except in this case." I smiled, reached over to the martini pitcher on the coffee table, and replenished her drink.

"Another toast," Mom said. "To picnics and the happiness they bring." Ruth was glowing as she brought the glass up and said, "L'Chaim."

Her mom was an unremarkable cook. The chicken breast with apricot sauce was okay, if a tad dry. The rice was inexplicably crunchy; I was afraid to ask if there were nuts in it. We all had a laugh when Ruth regaled us with the anecdote about how I had fooled her on the phone when pretending I was an investor from Oslo.

After satisfactory chocolate chip cookies, Ruth and her mother repaired to the garden. Dad filled a snifter with amber liquor, sat back, and regarded me. I let the breath flow into my abdomen, trying to savor the silence, which, as it appreciated, became scary.

"Ruth told me you were in the FBI," I offered. "I'll bet you have stories to tell."

"Not really," he shrugged. "Imagine James Bond, then conjure the opposite, if you will. I was a glorified pencil pusher."

"That's not what Ruth said. She said you were head of some wing with lots of power and intrigue."

"She speaks well of me because she loves me. The problem is I am afraid she is beginning to have strong feelings for you, too." I felt a small jolt, as if someone had lightly rear-ended my car.

"She's a good woman," I said.

He got up and ambled over to the fireplace, stared into the fire for a while. Then he turned.

"Paul, I love my daughter very much; she's my only child. Perhaps I have spoiled her, I don't know. It was easy to do because we loved her so much. Ruthie was, is, very, very sensitive. She needs to be with a man who reveres her; who is capable of giving and loving."

"I beg your—"

"Shut your face, Paul. Listen to me and listen well. When you leave this house, you will take my daughter home and you will kiss her and then you will tell her you're feeling ill. You will leave. You will then never call or see her again."

"But sir—"

He moved slightly closer.

"You care not a whit for my daughter. You can't care for anyone, why pretend. If you do not follow my instructions, I will destroy you and your business. I have friends who can do that as easily as turning a screw."

I sat there and permitted his words to penetrate. Ruthie and her mother returned, raving about forsythia. The three of them made light banter until it was time to leave. Mom and Dad sent us off as if they'd had the time of their lives.

On the ride home I wanted Ruth, maybe for the first time. I wanted to protect her, glorify her, tell her I loved her, that I would do anything for her. But I didn't. I followed her father's instructions to the T.

Because, you know, he was right.

THE JUMP

Two years after coming to LA to better my life, I found myself living in a cheap hotel room. The only redeeming feature was that it was a stone's throw from Tommy's, a 24-hour joint on Rampart I discovered had the best chili dogs in the Universe. That attribute notwithstanding, it was great to get a request from my friend Marcy to dog sit for a couple of days.

Marcy's La Cienega condo was magnificent, a 5th floor two-bedroom with a terrace that looked southeast over LA. On a smog free day, you could see the downtown skyline as clear as a postcard.

Her dog was a huge, sleek, auburn-colored creature named Delbert and my instructions were simple: feed and walk him twice a day, play ball as he enjoyed fetching, and give him love, lots of love, for Delbert needed love.

After several hours with the creature, I was convinced what he needed was time at an animal discipline school. He was a sweet animal. But he wouldn't leave me alone, following me around the apartment with a saliva-sodden tennis ball in his mouth, begging me with doleful eyes to toss it.

And toss I did. When my right arm got tired, I went to the left. By the middle of the week, I felt like an overworked relief pitcher in September.

On the morning of the fourth day, I awoke from a sleep interrupted countless times by Delbert's needs, made my way to the dining table, and tried to drink orange juice, read the *Racing Form*, and toss Delbert's ball at the same time.

I was near the edge when Delbert did the unforgivable. He slammed against the table spilling orange juice on the past performances.

As the newsprint sank into a pucker of wet paper, I fell into a silent rage. All the while I continued tossing the ball around the apartment … except I was throwing it closer to the terrace railing which Delbert, in his zeal to retrieve, would bang into, and lose his balance every time.

I don't know what made me do it. I don't think it was premeditated. I didn't hate the dog. I just lofted the ball in a low arch over the terrace railing. Delbert sprinted across the living room, took flight, and like a canine Lebron James sailed from the edge of the terrace, over the railing, and into the ether beyond.

Delbert's jump was so amazing that I yearned for a videotape replay. When one wasn't forthcoming, I rushed to the railing and peered over. There was Delbert, in the middle of the Olympic sized swimming pool, floating motionless like a hairy cork. He looked quite dead, neck no doubt broken from the impact of the 5-story fall.

I ran from the apartment. My thoughts were a blur. Did mouth to mouth resuscitation work on dogs? Was my passport up to date? What would I do with the body? Were there witnesses? Would I have to kill them, too?

I reached the pool and was just about to dive in when I realized it was empty. I was peering stupidly at the sun-dappled water when a sharp female voice apprehended me.

"You," it snapped. "You're the one who's taking care of Marcy's dog, aren't you?"

I turned to the voice and fell to my knees.

"Yes," I blubbered, "it was me. Please, I'm a good man and yet we all make mistakes …."

I was in the middle of my confession when a wet ball of auburn fur jumped into my arms and began licking my face. I held Delbert's very alive, wriggling body and licked him back. I don't know which one of us was whimpering louder.

For a day or two following the flight, Delbert wouldn't go near his water bowl. I had to drip water down his throat using a turkey baster. When he came around the rest of our time together was bliss. We played and played and I threw that ball until he was forced to rest.

A couple of weeks later, Marcy invited me for dinner. Delbert greeted me with tail wags and kisses and immediately trotted to the edge of the terrace. He sat staring at the railing as we ate dinner.

"He does that a lot," said Marcy. "He seems fascinated by the terrace."

That could be it, I thought. On the other hand, perhaps Delbert was contemplating another voyage. The excitement of exploration can do that to a soul. We yearn to explain the unexplained, solve the infinite mystery. Perhaps Delbert's tiny canine mind imagined a brave new world that featured flying hounds.

Thankfully, Delbert postponed his adventure until I finished my meal.

GOOD AND PROPER

I rarely read the paper, maybe once a month, so when I picked one up a picture on page two gave me a chill. It was the photograph of a cute young black girl with pigtails. The article described her as a retarded fourteen-year-old, missing for nearly three months. The parents, according to the article, were "sick with worry over their helpless daughter because of her condition," "deeply anguished," and "anxious for any information concerning their daughter's whereabouts." The article gave a hotline number and mentioned that the parents lived in Ellis Estates, a wealthy community on Long Island close to the Five Towns.

These people had serious money. I had worked as a gardener out at Ellis Estates a few summers earlier so I knew. I sat and pondered this and other things for a long time. After a while, I gathered up all the old magazines and newspapers in the house and cut out enough letters to spell out the following message:

YOU CAN HAVE YOUR DAUGHTER BACK FOR $10,000. 10's and 20's.

PUT THE MONEY IN A GREEN BOX AND LEAVE IT WITH THE CONCIERGE AT 1050 PARK AVENUE.

PUT FOR MR. HIRSCH ON THE OUTSIDE.

I put the message in an envelope and sent it to the worried parents, the rich, worried parents, on Long Island. Four days later, I sat across from 1050 Park Avenue in my cab, my attention seemingly on the *Racing Form*. In reality, I was watching for the bicycle messenger from the service I contacted to pick up the green box, green for money. He was to take it to the service desk at the Doral Hotel where I intended to pick it up later that evening.

Just after six, a cyclist with the name "Speed Demons" on a yellow shirt wheeled up. He leaned his bike against the building wall and walked into the entrance. He and the doorman started talking, the doorman punctuating his comments with waving arms. Finally, the messenger shrugged and walked out. Empty handed.

I could not believe it. The bastards had refused to pay off! I drove to the nearest phone and punched in the hotline number. A man answered on the first ring.

"Do you know your daughter's in danger? Where's the goddamn

cash?"

"W-who is this?"

"The guy with the green box. Where's the money?"

"How do we know… h-how… that you have any idea where our daughter is?"

"Trust, man, trust."

"I'm sorry, we can't do that. Without some kind of proof, it's impossible. Do you know how many calls we've had?"

I smashed the receiver down. Sonofabitch. I should have known they were going to ask for proof. Nothing came easy in this world.

I drove home and got out the bottle of Dewar's. After I put away several shots I unlocked the basement door and went down to my soundproof workshop that I had converted into a playroom.

She was in the corner playing with her Barbies. When she saw me, her face lit up and she rushed to me. I held her in my arms and played with her pigtails. The photograph in the paper hadn't captured her true beauty. She hugged me and yelled unintelligible things into my ear.

I hadn't meant to keep her when I found her wandering around the mall. But she had become so much to me, a daughter, a friend, a bit of warmth in a cold, joyless life.

After a while she crawled back to her dolls. I had her hold a copy of a newspaper with today's date circled on the front page. I snapped the picture. At least the parents would know I had her. I sent them the picture and new instructions for delivering the money, this time for $20,000.

With that kind of dough, I could raise her good and proper.

PARABLE

The fat man let me into his world in slow and subtle ways. One day he began calling me by my first name. Soon after, he started talking to me about the fine art of shooting pool. The fat man could play the hell out of that game. He could barely bend over the table but with a smooth stroke knocked the balls into the pockets with unerring accuracy. When he missed a shot, it was almost as if he wanted to.

Sometimes it was tough to make sense of the fat man's words. They were like puzzles. It was rumored the fat man spent time in the orient working with a key Buddhist guy. Maybe that accounted for it. One day the fat man and I were playing a game of straight pool. I missed an easy shot and cursed.

"Don't try to read the book," said the fat man. "Grow a beard and fart instead." I asked him to elaborate.

"I never saw a chimney that didn't amuse me," he said. "All that smoke running upward, onward, defying gravity and disappearing. That's what pool is about. Defying everything there is inside you that makes it possible to miss a shot like you just missed."

About a year later when my game was strong, I hustled an inferior opponent into a game of nine ball. For some reason, I played poorly from the outset but never thought of stopping the game, assuming that my true talent would reveal itself. I quit when I was broke and nobody in the poolroom would lend me another cent. That night I decided that my love for the game of pool wasn't worth the humiliation and financial ruin that was possible in competition. I never picked up a pool cue again.

I chose to invest my money in more worthwhile propositions, like taking women out to eat and purchasing an occasional CD's. I spent very little time up at the pool hall and saw the fat man less and less.

As time went on, I found I was doing things I never could have imagined as a youth. I got a nine-to-five job, began to need women for companionship rather than to satisfy a sexual craving, and stopped inquiring into the nature of things. Circumstances seemed to create my being and not the other way around.

I found it was easier not to shave in the morning and grew a beard. I read very little and farted every chance I got.

TREPIDATION

"Do you not know the meaning of the word trepidation?" she asked one day as she was brushing her hair with a steam shovel.

"Not know? I invented the word, Sylvia. I live it. I embody it. Now pass the trellis."

She gathered up her long skirts and there was one left on the ground. Though I felt sorry for it I deigned to put it on.

She walked trotted, cantered, galloped and ascended to her horse and you know what the latter did. I ran after her but could not keep up with the fair steed as I was wearing manacles. Oh time, you beast.

I knelt by the water and stared into it. I thought about jumping in and ending it all but it was just a puddle, the circumference of a large pizza. Pizza is good. It interests me to say that. I looked toward the mountains. I looked toward the sea. I looked to the river and slapped my knee. Knee diggy diggy dig. Knee diggy dig. Yip yip diggy diggy. Yip diggy dig.

I danced and sang until coyotes ran from their natural habitats, tails between their legs, and squirrels skydived and birds befriended worms …

… and still no Sylvia. Each day I put my ear to the ground to see if I could discern the return of her mighty steed but all I heard were arguments among the ants. "Stop bumping into me," seemed to be the common lament.

I knitted, I rose at dawn, I scoured the campsite. I called imaginary friends and I wrote twig symphonies. Have you ever played the twigs? Liar.

I began to collude with my depressive qualities. I snuck away and soiled myself—yes. Then I clutched a tree and kissed the bark and begged, entreated it. "I am not Sylvia, release me," a little leaf screeched.

Sylvia was right, of course, had been right all along. She needed someone stronger, someone with a nose for adventure; a prince, not a dwarf.

When the rains came, I found myself trying to build a fire using toe and fingernails for tinder. I had just elicited a small spark from my nearly dormant passion when the lid blew and a torrent of rain carried me swiftly to the place I had always been. I had trusted, that was the problem. You can't find a good hideaway these days, not with no ego down.

Sitting, sitting, bereft of desire or illusion, contemplating the beyond and the back again of never, I saw into her eyes, her soul, cavorting in space and I knew, I knew, I knew.

I took a step toward the perimeter.

THE GREAT TRUTH

He looked like a little Jewish Buddha. He had to be pushing ninety. He was married to a woman who was some relation to the host of this Rosh Hashanah dinner.

Time had reduced him to about five feet and a hundred pounds. His wispy grey hair was combed neatly left to right. He was dressed sharp: blue blazer, starched white shirt, tie, fresh pressed grey slacks, shiny shoes. He leaned over, plunged a cracker into a mound of homemade chopped liver, and guided it into his mouth. He chewed as if eating was a meditation. We were seated in easy chairs about three feet apart. Most of the attendees were in a corner, cooing over a newborn baby and catching up. I didn't want to be at this extravaganza or anywhere, except maybe the racetrack. For some reason, I had a desire to talk with the old man.

"How are you?" I asked.

"Vat?"

"How-are-you-doing?" I said, louder.

"Goot. Okay."

"Great chopped liver," I said.

"Goot. Very goot." As he spoke bits of liver hopped off his tongue and stuck to his lips.

"What have you been up to?"

"Not much."

"You watch TV?" This is the first question I ask anybody.

"A little."

"What do you watch? The news?"

"Maybe de news. Maybe anudda program."

"You have a TV in the bedroom?"

"No."

"You're kidding."

"No. No."

"Don't you like watching TV lying down?"

"No."

"Just before going to sleep?"

"No."

"Where do you watch?"

"Ve have two sets."

I was impressed. "Two! Where?"

"In de living room."

"But you can't watch them at the same time."

"Ve do."

"It must get noisy."

"No. The den goes dis vay. She vatches one, I watch de udda."

"Your wife?"

"No, my girlfriend. Oh course, my vife!"

I smiled. For a while we concentrated on putting a dent in the mountain of chopped liver.

"What kind of work did you do?" I asked.

"Bakery."

"You were a baker?"

"No. No."

"Owner?"

"Yes. I owned the shop."

"What was the name?"

"I don't remember."

"Good pastries?"

"Very goot. Yes."

I thought about éclairs and Napoleons. This guy was a deity. I leaned forward.

"Say. What's the most important thing you have learned from life? The great truth."

"Dat I have survived."

"You survived. That's it?"

"I vas in Germany, Russia, Palestine, very difficult times. That I made it here to dis great country and am alive today is de most important ting. I have survived. Survived!"

While I was pondering this nugget, his wife, a bag of grimaces and bones, sat down in a chair next to him. She placed a hand on top of his.

"Fifty years," she said. "Fifty years ve have been together."

"Congratulations," I said.

"I luf him so much, you know. Except now he doesn't remember a ting. It's like living vit a table."

"Really," I said.

"It's been difficult lately, cleaning the vounds on his feet. The diabetes, you know. I can't let him out of the house even. He gets lost. The police had to find him twice last month. I do everyting, the shopping, cooking, dressing. Mommy has to take care of you, isn't that right?" She leaned over and kissed the top of his head.

"And look at dis." She picked pieces of chopped liver off his lips, placed them on her index finger, and shoved them into his mouth. "My bubbala can't even eat anymore." The old man seemed to be shrinking, disappearing into himself.

"He is my little baby now. He never gave me a baby, you know. So, dis is how it is."

I couldn't believe how she was infantilizing him. I wouldn't have been surprised if she whipped a bottle of formula out of her purse.

"I vas surprised to see him talking to you. He doesn't talk to many people. He likes you."

"He's an amazing guy," I said. I leaned over and tapped his knee. "We were just talking about life, weren't we?"

He opened his mouth but nothing came out. His legs spread and his ass lifted off the couch. A large fart and huge stench filled the air.

"Oh, you," she said. "Look vat you did. You made a poopy, here at the Rosh Hashanah dinner."

She slapped the top of his head. "It's a good ting I brought extra diapers." She yanked him to his feet and pulled him toward the bathroom.

Dinner was announced. As I prepared to join the others I thought about the importance of survival.

DISAPPEARANCE

I brought the information on my little catering company to printers named "Pincus and Salazzi." I met with Hyman Pincus, one of the owners. He was a kindly, older gentleman. He said his company would take my ideas and create a lovely brochure. His manner inspired trust.

About two weeks later, I received a call that the brochures were ready. Pincus greeted me at the door and put a bony arm around my waist.

"You're going to love 'em," he said.

Once seated, he produced a brochure and placed it on a desk. It was indeed gorgeous. As I flipped through, I realized the book captured my company's intent ... until the last page. There, on the back cover were huge block letters reading:

PINCUS & SALAZZI PRODUCTIONS

CALL 1 800 421 PINSAL

I quickly went back through the brochure, afraid to confirm a dark suspicion. It was confirmed. My company name and phone number were nowhere to be found! Only information on Pincus and Salazzi occurred at random intervals.

"How do you like it?" Pincus asked.

"It's beautiful," I said. "Except there's no mention of my company. Just yours." Pincus rifled through the brochure.

"You're right," he said. "Your number isn't listed. I guess we thought it would be better if your clients went through us."

"But it's my company!"

"Sure it is, Mr. Geffling. But we're partners now and it's better for everybody in the long run."

I got to my feet. "Mr. Pincus, I appreciate your efforts. But I don't think I'll be needing your services."

"Come on," he said putting a bony arm on mine. "Fred and Ginger, Martin and Lewis, Abbott and Costello, raisins and bran. Partnerships are the key the success."

I roughly brushed him off. He winced. "If that's the way you want it," he said, "Perhaps it's time to meet Mr. Salazzi."

He pressed a red button on the desk. Seconds later in strolled a swarthy, mustachioed man who would have fit right into a Godfather movie. He sat down next to me.

"Carmine Salazzi, how you doing?" he said. He extended a thick, manicured hand which featured a huge diamond pinky ring.

"Not so good, Mr. Salazzi," I said, shaking his hand. I was aware of great strength in his grip. "I came to get my brochure and now you want to be my partner."

"He hurt my arm," said Pincus.

"No shit," said Salazzi. "Why'd you do that, paisan?" He gave my hand a squeeze. The pain shot up my arm like electricity.

"I-I- I didn't mean to hurt him," I said. "Maybe it's my trust issues regarding money as a replacement for love but, after all, you're taking my company—"

"Shut up, ya little fuck," said Salazzi. "You come to us, remember? You come through that door, you make the commitment. Nobody backs out of a commitment to Pincus and Salazzi. Capiche?"

An abject confusion had me paralyzed. From a distance, I heard a gurgling sound come from my mouth.

"I'll take that as a yes," said Salazzi. "It's gonna be a perfect relationship. And if you get the bright idea to go to the cops I'll pound you like a heavy bag at the gym. I bet you wouldn't enjoy sipping your meals through a straw."

Pincus slid a thick contract across the desk. I wavered for a moment until Salazzi opened his sharkskin sport coat and I saw the silver handle of a gun sticking out of his waistband.

After a few months, even my most loyal clients stopped calling me. I'd drop into Pincus and Salazzi every morning to see if there was anything I could do. Over espresso and donuts, Pincus would tell me they had it under control.

One night, I went home and discovered Salazzi in bed with my girlfriend. Don't worry, he said, he'd make me proud. I shrugged and packed some toiletries and went to a motel.

Sometime later, I received a phone call from Pincus at the flophouse where I was staying, telling me to come into the office. When I arrived, sitting there with Pincus and Salazzi was a guy who could have been my brother. The resemblance was that striking.

"Whaddaya think, Mr. Geffling. Not bad, huh?" grinned Salazzi.

I had to agree. It appeared that they had decided to substitute for me altogether.

ASIAN GRANDMA

Now that I am enlightened I can accept, with some equanimity, that my partner, who has been on vacation for four days, has not called me this morning. This is not my biggest problem. It is my imminent death from eating horrifying foods for many years. I saw an acupuncturist in the late 80's. Amazing woman named Trinh Le. She had me write down everything I ate for a week. When she read the list, she screamed, "Oh my God! This can't be! How are you alive?"

Although Trinh Le was a wizard with the needles (notwithstanding the time she left a needle in my forehead and I almost gave myself a lobotomy when, while driving home from a session, I tried swatting a fly) a lot more happened during treatment. During the forty-five minute sessions, she would talk with me about my life. Her words gave me hope, that most precious commodity. If I moaned about killing so many animals to feed the multitude at the corporate picnics my company provided, she would say, in her sing-song voice, "You make people happy. Make children smile. You have good business. It support you. You do good thing."

Trinh Le was referred to me by a yoga instructor in Hollywood, a lovely woman with an odd hairdo that featured several snake-like strands adhered to her forehead by a translucent glue. I never got yoga. I couldn't grasp there was no winning and losing, that if the woman next to me stretched a little farther or held a pose longer, I wouldn't drop in the standings.

Trinh Le had her practice in a small house in West LA. She weighed no more than ninety pounds. At the time I met her, I was resigned to being in a wheelchair in the not too distant future. My neck and back hurt constantly.

The sessions started with my lying face down on the table and Trinh Le playing pin the tail on Jim. Most of the needles went in easily but several, such as those in my lips, toes, and ears, got my attention. She would occasionally attach the needles to electrodes leading to a small generator, sending electrical current into the area in an effort to increase blood flow. After the mini-electrocutions I would fall into the deepest sleep. After removing the needles Trinh Le would massage and talk to me.

"You have wonderful body, very strong, you have no problem," she said. And I knew she was telling the truth. Maybe it was the needles, her words, or her confidence in my recovery, but I started to heal. Trinh Le became more than an acupuncturist. She became a living grandmother. Family.

I would tell her about my lifelong desire to beat the horse races. Trinh Le said, "Oh, no good. You have so much, a good business, a good woman, a nice life. Why horses? You want to win too badly and you afraid to lose, too. Poor you. You keep going to racetrack you have stroke one day and then you be crying forever."

Trinh Le had the stroke first. For a while I would call or stop by. One of her daughters would answer and politely tell me Trinh Le wasn't seeing visitors, but that she sent everybody her love.

FIVE SECRETS

"Every person has five secrets," she said. I was trying to find the Jets game on her TV. Since she received maybe ten channels—she claimed it was some kind of homeowners rule—I wasn't having much luck.

"Five secrets," she repeated. "During the course of a relationship, it is the task of one's mate to discover these secrets. That is the key to happiness and longevity in a relationship."

The best I could do was the *Home Shopping Network*. They were selling earrings that appeared encrusted with real diamonds, though for $29.95 it didn't seem likely.

"A lot of women revere diamonds," I mused. "They sometimes mistake the glitter of minerals for true love."

I waited for a response. She sat on the bed staring at her lap. She was big on yoga and I admired her ability to get into positions I couldn't achieve even as a flexible child. She sat with a straight back and legs folded Indian style.

"One down, four to go," she said.

That's right, I thought, four stations left to find the football game. I stumbled across the *Ellen Degeneres* show. Ellen was giving away a mountain of blenders, TVs and iPads to a screaming audience, some of whom were foaming at the mouth. I liked Ellen, she seemed sincere.

"You know," I said, "great performers don't have to memorize their lines. What we hear from them aren't words but the essence of who they are. When you think about it, communication is nothing more the sharing of one's truth."

She sighed. Got up from the bed, leaned over, shook her hair, stood up, and it fell into place. Even when I had hair I needed a horse brush and helmet to tame it.

"Two down, three to go," she said. I reached for the remote. "No, she said, "no more channels, for today. I must protect my remaining three secrets."

Secrets, I heard her say. What secrets?

THE LOSS

When I stepped on the scale and saw that I weighed 230 pounds, I knew I had to do something. Some linebackers look great with 230 pounds stretched across their skin like a painter's canvas. My 230 pounds made me look like a huge mound of frozen custard. Unclothed and standing, my stomach occluded a view of my magnificent genitalia.

What finally got me going was the obsession that if I became fat free I might actually have sex. Celibacy was wearing me out.

My program consisted of one raw egg in the morning, a glass of carrot juice at lunch, and a slab of broiled fish for dinner. I drank water until I thought I'd sprout gills and ate more vitamins than Linus Pauling. My daily regimen included 3 miles of jogging, 100 sit-ups, and 100 push-ups.

During the first week, I was ravenous and almost fainted while watching a Hostess cake commercial. The solution was to chew an evil tasting B-12 vitamin every time I thought of food.

It took two months to get down to 190 pounds. Though there was still a miniMichelin around the waist, it was a lot better than when I started.

I tried to resume a normal life but could not. The need to be perfect spurred me on. I bought designer threads when I reached a rock hard 180 pounds. I tanned until I looked undocumented. At a salon on Rodeo Drive I got a $200 hair styling instead of the $6 Barber College special. I purchased blue-tinted contact lenses and had my teeth whitened until they glistened like linoleum tiles. A woman waxed me until I was as hairless as a newt.

Three months later, I stared in the mirror. I was beyond beautiful. I had become the male version of the woman who would never date me. It was time to share myself with the world.

I took women out to eat. They were beautiful, charming, and attracted to me. Yet as they talked, I found myself gazing at my reflection in whatever piece of stainless steel happened to be at the table. When one invited me back to her house, I furtively did 200 push-ups as she made us martinis.

I was troubled by my lack of interest in the opposite sex until one day, while spraying myself with emollients I realized that nobody appealed to me except ... me. I had fallen in love with myself!

There were advantages. I would always be home when I called. I'd save on meals. No one felt better to me than me. And the only person I could ever blame for a bad date would be me. Hell, I could do a lot worse than me.

With arms folded, each hand caressing a bulging bicep, I took myself to a favorite restaurant for piece of flounder.

HORROR

After a lifetime of feeling as if he didn't belong, of being an outsider, the realization that he was being rejected by the world's most forgiving and accepting body was, to say the least, hurtful.

So as not to feel as if he was participating in this exclusion, he made an effort to sit in the physical center of the rooms in which the meetings were held. With a courage that made him dizzy, he introduced himself to people and extended his hand to newcomers. He volunteered for any act of service: cleaning up, offering literature, or attending meetings on the West Side that dealt with the group's international agenda.

He raised his hand often and spoke from the heart as best he could. He made an effort to communicate with himself while sharing, so the monstrous ego would be kept at bay and the articulation of his reality would have nothing to do with the need to impress others.

He made a special point of being well groomed. He wore fresh clothes, shaved and showered every day, polished his teeth and car, and chewed minty gum until his jaw ached. He did the things his sponsor told him to do and when the rage came up, the rage that emanated from his feeling of being excluded, of being herded from this new experience as he had been separated from all that was nurturing his entire life, he meditated on it and tried to release it.

Nobody talked to him and rarely was a phone call returned, even by his mentor, or sponsor.

After he shared, sometimes the group would not applaud, as they did out of politeness for even the most disgusting outcasts. And during cleanup at the end of the meetings, not even the unkempt losers with coffee grounds stuck to their fingertips would make so much as casual conversation.

Wasn't this what the program was not about? Wasn't the program about forgiveness, love, about making amends when you were wrong? Wasn't this supposed to be about surrender and acceptance and loss of ego and unanimity, hell, wasn't unity the essence of it?

His brother, who tolerated him, took him to a party in Seal Beach one Sunday afternoon. While most of the beautiful people lolled on the beach displaying their gym-toned, sun block greased bodies, the owner of the house took him on a tour and displayed his massive gun collection.

He gazed upon row after row of gleaming black, navy blue, and gray weapons of destruction, grenades, silencers, assault weapons, derringers, pistols, some metal, some plastic. It went on and on, a stolid, motionless field of death. The man had just purchased a highly-valued semi-automatic rifle, a weapon capable of firing many rounds per second. It was a duplicate of a gun that had entered his collection via another supplier. Would he like to buy it? It was a beauty, a mayhem maker, as the man called it.

He held the gun in his arms, hefted the five cold pounds of it, went to the window and sighted, first on the distant horizon, then the swooping gulls, the surfers and, finally, the groups of party-goers. He pressed the trigger, heard the click, and paid the $800. The man wrapped the gun in a crinkly Rite Aid bag, clapped him on the back, and congratulated him on a fine choice.

At the meeting that night a pretty girl described how her boyfriend had yelled at her in public, called her a fool and threatened to leave. As if that wasn't bad enough her AIDS test had come back positive, library job of ten years terminated, and cat flattened by a UPS truck. He approached her after the meeting, introduced himself, and told her his heart went out to her. She stared at him, through him, said thanks, and walked away.

He went through the motions of putting chairs away, smiled the obligatory smile. He asked to speak to his sponsor but the sponsor was in a rush, didn't have time to talk. He walked outside and observed the groups of chatting, laughing, smiling members, looking for all the world as if they were at a party, a party to which he was once again uninvited.

He walked to his car and opened the trunk. For a long time, he stared at the weapon. He prayed: "God, I'm very confused. I know I'm supposed to do your will, but why am I so left out? Why can't be part of things? Why don't people like me, I try to do the right things. Please help me, God. Please, God, please, let me do your will. Please."

PIANO PLAYER

My girlfriend needed a lock of my hair. I let her cut it off. She put it on the altar in the corner of our bedroom which was adorned with an assortment of amulets, potions, and dried animal parts. The fact that my girlfriend was a witch didn't bother me. My neighbor's piano playing was much more problematic. Day after day I would listen to him practicing scales over and over, a repetition that conjured the torture of memorizing algorithms in high school.

"Maybe you can put a spell on our neighbor," I said to my sweetheart.

"I can only use my powers for good," she said.

Later that day I went out to get the racing paper and Chinese food. My fiancée had gone to the massage parlor. She claimed she gave therapeutic massages. I doubted that. Her mouth was a vacuum cleaner and there was no way she was pulling in $400 a day with toe twisting and muscle kneading. But cash was cash.

I was coming down the hall when I passed my neighbor's door. I stopped. Do re mi fa so what the fuck. I rang the doorbell. The scales stopped and I waited, the roast duck wonton cooling by the second.

"Who is it?" said a woman's voice.

"It's your next-door neighbor in 4H, Sid Lubitz."

"Oh, hold on." A multitude of locks clicked and the door opened to reveal a young woman who could have been on the cover of a man's magazine. She was wearing a yellow sundress more blinding than the sun.

"Why hello, Mr Lubitz."

"You can call me Sid."

"Hello, Sid, I don't think we've met. I'm Lila Thomas."

"Hello, Lila." She took my hand. Held it for a couple of seconds after I relaxed my grip.

"I was wondering. The piano. I thought it was your husband."

"Yes," she said. "My husband's the real player but … we've been separated for about a month. It takes my mind off things. I hope it's not bothering you."

"Bother?" I said. "I've never heard better scales in my life. Putzini couldn't play better scales."

"Putzini?"

"Bernardo Putzini, the great tenor pianist from the Grand Concourse. I have an old tape if you want."

"That's okay," she smiled. Her teeth were even and white. "Would you like to come in? I've just made a pot of coffee."

When I got back home I wasn't sad that I missed that afternoon's TV shows. It was one of the best days of my life. When my wife got back we played a game of cribbage. There was something missing but I couldn't put my finger on it. Later, just before going to sleep, it hit me.

There was no piano playing coming from Lila's apartment. Or the next day or the next. On the morning of the third day I rang Lila's bell and when there was no answer I called the manager. They had to break down the door. The apartment was starting to stink. The coroner said it was a heart attack.

A couple of weeks later I woke to find my wife clipping my toenails. "For the altar," she said.

"Are you sure you're using your powers for good?" I asked.

"Oh yes, darling," she said. "For *our* good."

After we broke up, I put as many miles between that woman and myself as possible.

I discovered, over time, that it is impossible to outrun a witch's spell.

THE DRAGON

Very few women responded to his over-fifty on-line dating ad. His photos were of a rather plain, bald, bespectacled, a man well into his sixties. The vanished dreams of youth were evident in the dull, button eyes. Errant culinary choices manifested in the distended belly. Looking at his soft lips of little character, it was hard to see what kind of woman could respond. His bio was not enticing. He had worked in the event planning business and was semi-retired. He enjoyed watching sports and movies on TV, fast food, and going to the racetrack.

The world is filled with many women. It may be, in the Dating Universe, there is a match for everyone. Several women contacted him. They met for coffee. He had worked on being non-judgmental. Yet it was hard not to judge these women. They were older than their photos. One had on so much lipstick that by the time she finished her coffee the rim of the cup was slathered with a crimson sludge. Another coughed up phlegm into a tattered Kleenex, insisting the antibiotics were working and there was no need to worry. One seemed normal until she described disillusion with divorced husband of forty years, and mimicked stabbing him by lifting an imaginary knife over her head and bringing it down, over and over into her stomach. He attempted to rise to the level of being interested and interesting, without success. He knew he wasn't a great catch. He was just looking for someone to whom he was attracted, someone with whom he could share his waning libido who did not charge two hundred dollars.

He was to discover what many have learned: the moment you give up—the possibility of attainment occurs. He surrendered in his apartment. He was eating two undercooked sweet potatoes while watching the young Lakers win the opening game of the season when he realized that he would be alone forever. There was no more love for him. He put his paper plate down and sobbed. I will be better by myself, he thought. This is the will of God.

At that moment of surrender the mail alert on his laptop dinged. He went online. It was from the dating site. A pretty woman was responding to his ad. Her message: "You have told me all I need to know. I would like to meet you. I need a man to slay the dragon."

His first thought was that she was crazy. The second, who cares. Forgetting that moments ago he had resigned himself to a monastic existence he shot back a reply. "It is so good to hear from you. I have not slain a dragon in a while. My sword is dull but it is long and my spirit is willing." As he was rebuking himself for such an idiotic reply, she messaged that she would like him to come to her house for their first date.

As he drove to her place high up in the mountains of Topanga, a part of LA with which he was unfamiliar, he had flowers on the passenger seat and grim anticipation in his heart. Skidding bursts of grey clouds darkened the afternoon sky. Sodium lamps popped on, casting ghostly shadows over Pacific Coast Highway. Large, strange birds cawed and swooped in wide circles close to his windshield. Out of the corners of his eyes, he thought he saw diminutive humans scuttling like vermin along the sides of the road.

When he reached her small house, he felt as if he had run a marathon. She was as pretty as her online photos. She accepted the flowers with a glistening smile. She led him to a lounge chair into which he sank. The moment he did so, handcuffs sprang out of the sides, pinning his wrists to the armrests.

He knew he was going to die. It did not matter. There was no point in living. He had squandered his chances. All he yearned for was to have someone stand up for him, to rally to his defense, a child, a mate, an organization who could prove his worth and justify his existence. There was no one. She held his hand and described the injections. The first to relax, then paralyze, then stop the heart.

"What about the dragon?" he asked, surprised he was curious about anything.

"Don't worry," she said. "You will get your chance to slay it."

OUR SON

Driving north on the Merritt Parkway all twists and turns, stark winter driven trees a lurching canopy under which we speed, and the circuitous road reminds me of unpredictable events that have led us to this tipping point, my wife beside me, son in the back seat behind her.

He is wordless, my son, staring out the window, peering at this loveless winter: small tidy houses tucked behind fir and evergreen, polished cars sentry-like before snow slaked lawns, a firmament suggesting placid normalcy that has evaded him; he a polliwog doomed to remain unformed, wriggling, purposeless, and although I harbor faint hope this journey may be one of redemption, my heart knows better.

The destination is a mental institution named, curiously, High Point, and we must secrete our son there, our son, for he has become a nuisance, an embarrassment, and this cannot be countenanced. Our family must never yield to the temptation of its vices, murmurs or muted assent strewn and torn asunder by screams of reprisal that reach up, grasping, twisted hands clawing for purchase beneath a sea of molten admonition. This is my son, the son who almost was, and he is separating from his peers, fine boys who sing hymns in tune, harmonious all in the choir of conformity and who, for the most part, cling to the idea of ambition. If I could have taught my son anything it would have been to be a good boy or at least make a show of it. That's what makes this thing work, it's the mortar and pestle of this tricky house of sticks we call society. Enjoy laughter with others or at others but not at yourself, at least until the clackety sound of mirth loses the power to rend crisp the rich fat of hope. I think of a thin and flimsy swan, marked for death by the flock which knows better than to tolerate the grisly difference which imperils.

My son had a chance; we gave him every opportunity. He squandered it, as a hobo would a fortune, on inebriants and the dubious comfort of another drunk. I should perhaps blame the wall of false pride behind which so many of the young cower.

I look at my son's reflection through the rearview, my son, who will shortly be my son no more, and for a moment my fingers twitch with the need to reach out, as if by touching him I can restore innocence

and imbue sweet, brown eyes with joy and trust.
 The feeling passes quick, a leaf blown across this devil's parkway by an unforgiving wind.

Manufactured by Amazon.ca
Acheson, AB

33282980R00090